# A SAFARI OF THE MIND

# A SAFARI OF THE MIND

Mike Resnick

Wildside Press
New Jersey • 1999

A SAFARI OF THE MIND





ISBN 1-58715-006-9 (trade paperback)
ISBN 1-58715-007-7 (hardcover)

FIRST EDITION

# Contents

To Carol, as always

And to John Betancourt—
always Johnny-on-the-spot
when I need a publisher

# INTRODUCTION

## by Kristine Kathryn Rusch

He calls my husband "the golf geek" and then promises to take me away to exotic places. First, an elephant-back safari in Africa, then a marvelous hut built on stilts over the ocean in Bora Bora. And then, of course, he reminds me that he must bring his wife, Carol.

He, of course, is Mike Resnick and beneath that teasing, flirtatious tone is one of the most intense men I've ever met. Mike started out as a science fiction fan, and has a great love for the genre, but that doesn't stop him from being one of the best businessmen I've ever known.

When I was editing *The Magazine of Fantasy and Science Fiction*, he would occasionally call and say, "Beautiful," (writers can go far calling an editor beautiful) "I just finished an award-winning novella. If you'd like to see it, you got twenty-four hours to let me know if you're going to buy it."

Now, when most professional writers say a story is award-quality, they're fooling themselves. Very few professional writers are good judges of their own work. Mike is one of those few. Every single story he pitched to me as an award winner when I was his editor won an award. Every single one. No other writer ever achieved that. And because he knew the quality of his work, he knew its worth. I'm glad I no longer sit across the negotiating desk from Mr. Mike Resnick. I'm not that savvy an operator.

However, that doesn't stop me from taking lessons. Mike is free with advice to folks whom he believes will benefit from it. In fact, he's one of the most generous people I know. He gives out story ideas like they're candy, collaborates with everyone under the sun, and will recommend friends for projects if those friends happen to be perfect for the job.

When he edited a series of anthologies a few years ago, he was, by far, the best editor in the business. He suggested stories to folks who couldn't think any up, and he had cogent comments for folks whose stories needed revision, and he discovered fine new writers like Nick DiChario. He never turned any good story away, and so some of those anthologies ballooned to twice their suggested size. Mike is the only person I know who has lost money editing—because he believed the work was so important that he would pay for something out of his own pocket if the project was overbudget. Of course, every anthology had a Resnick story and there are some of those included in here. Some show Mike's terrific sense of humor (something that has served him well in Hollywood. Maybe someday he'll write those memoirs, and people will get to hear his tales of strangeness and woe from LaLa Land); others show why Mike often had the best story in his own anthology. The award winners are well represented here too, including "Seven Views of Olduvai Gorge" which happens to be one of those stories that Mike gave me exactly 24 hours to declare acceptable which, of course, I did. There was no way I'd ever turn my back on a Resnick story, even if it wasn't a guaranteed award winner. Mike is one of our best writers, and the stories in this collection prove that. So I let him make his empty promises and insult my husband (with whom he always plans silly & successful projects) and I tell him I'll go to Africa or Bora Bora with him and Carol as long as I can bring the golf geek.

Because being with Mike is like reading a Resnick story. You never know what's going to happen next.

## Introduction to "Seven Views of Olduvai Gorge"

The seed for "Seven Views of Olduvai Gorge" was sown one hot September day in Botswana, when Carol and I were on safari. She and our driver happened to see a spring hare—an African rabbit —and we pulled to a stop so the two of them could observe and discuss it. There were a hundred elephants just over the next hill. I could hear them; hell, I could even smell them—but I couldn't interest Carol or the driver in leaving the spring hare just yet. And I muttered something like, "Who comes to Africa just to look at a goddamned rabbit?" And it suddenly occured to me that, between poaching and habitat destruction, the day was perhaps not long off when that was precisely what people would come to Africa to see, and I decided to write the story when I got home.

Well, the safari lasted another five weeks, and by the time we arrived home I had another future safari story to tell. And Carol suggested a third riff on the theme, and we spent a few months discussing it while I wrote other things, and suddenly I had an eons-long Stapledonian story that could be set in one location in Africa.

I hate to sound too immodest, but I knew as I was writing it that "Seven Views of Olduvai Gorge" was something special. The first people to see it were the judges of the Universitat Politecnica de Catalunya Contest, an annual big-money prize in Spain for the best science fiction novella of the year. I submitted it under a pseudonym (as per the rules, so the judges couldn't be influenced by the author's name) and it won, which implies a certain universality of theme, since none of the judges were American.

Then it won the Nebula (my first), the Science Fiction Chronicle Poll (my fifth), the HOMer Award (my fourth), and the Hugo (my third). Four years later it's still making its way around the world and still winning awards, most recently the Ignotus Award (the Spanish Hugo), the Futura Award (Croatia), and the Prix Ozone (France).

# SEVEN VIEWS OF OLDUVAI GORGE

The creatures came again last night.

The moon had just slipped behind the clouds when we heard the first rustlings in the grass. Then there was a moment of utter silence, as if they knew we were listening for them, and finally there were the familiar hoots and shrieks as they raced to within fifty meters of us and, still screeching, struck postures of aggression.

They fascinate me, for they never show themselves in the daylight, and yet they manifest none of the features of the true nocturnal animal. Their eyes are not oversized, their ears cannot move independently, they tread very heavily on their feet. They frighten most of the other members of my party, and while I am curious about them, I have yet to absorb one of them and study it.

To tell the truth, I think my use of absorption terrifies my companions more than the creatures do, though there is no reason why it should. Although I am relatively young by my race's standards, I am nevertheless many millennia older than any other member of my party. You would think, given their backgrounds, that they would know that any trait someone of my age possesses must by definition be a survival trait.

Still, it bothers them. Indeed, it *mystifies* them, much as my memory does. Of course, theirs seem very inefficient to me. Imagine having to learn everything one knows in a single lifetime, to be totally ignorant at the moment of birth! Far better to split off from your parent with his knowledge intact in your brain, just as my parent's knowledge came to him, and ultimately to me.

But then, that is why we are here: not to compare similarities, but to study differences. And never was there a race so different from all his fellows as Man. He was extinct barely seventeen millennia after he strode boldly out into the galaxy from this, the planet of his birth—but during that brief interval he wrote a chapter in galactic history that will last forever. He claimed the stars for his own, colonized a million worlds, ruled his empire with an iron will. He gave no quarter during his primacy, and he asked for none during his decline and fall. Even now, some forty-eight centuries after his extinction, his accomplishments and his failures still excite the imagination.

Which is why we are on Earth, at the very spot that was said to be Man's true birthplace, the rocky gorge where he first crossed over the evolutionary barrier, saw the stars with fresh eyes, and vowed that they would someday be his.

Our leader is Bellidore, an Elder of the Kragan people, orange-skinned, golden-fleeced, with wise, patient ways. Bellidore is well-versed in the behavior of sentient beings, and settles our disputes before we even know that we are engaged in them.

Then there are the Stardust Twins, glittering silver beings who answer to each other's names and finish each other's thoughts. They have worked on seventeen archaeological digs, but even *they* were surprised when Bellidore chose them for this most prestigious of all missions. They behave like life mates, though they display no sexual characteristics—but like all the others, they refuse to have physical contact with me, so I cannot assuage my curiosity.

Also in our party is the Moriteu, who eats the dirt as if it were a delicacy, speaks to no one, and sleeps upside-down while hanging from a branch of a nearby tree. For some reason, the creatures always leave it alone. Perhaps they think it is dead, possibly they know it is asleep and that only the rays of the sun can awaken it. Whatever the reason, we would be lost without it, for only the delicate tendrils that extend from its mouth can excavate the ancient artifacts we have discovered with the proper care.

We have four other species with us: one is an Historian, one an Exobiologist, one an Appraiser of human artifacts, and one a Mystic. (At least, I *assume* she is a Mystic, for I can find no pattern to her approach, but this may be due to my own shortsightedness. After all, what I do seems like magic to my companions and yet it is a rigorously-applied science.)

And, finally, there is me. I have no name, for my people do not use names, but for the convenience of the party I have taken the name of He Who Views for the duration of the expedition. This is a double misnomer: I am not a *he*, for my race is not divided by gender; and I am not a viewer, but a Fourth Level Feeler. Still, I could intuit very early in the voyage that "feel" means something very different to my companions than to myself, and out of respect for their sensitivities, I chose a less accurate name.

Every day finds us back at work, examining the various strata. There are many signs that the area once teemed with living things, that early on there was a veritable explosion of life forms in this place, but very little remains today. There are a few species of insects and birds, some small rodents, and of course the creatures who visit our camp nightly.

Our collection has been growing slowly. It is fascinating to watch my companions perform their tasks, for in many ways they are as much of a mystery to me as my methods are to them. For example, our Exobiologist needs only to glide her tentacle across an object to tell us whether it was once living matter; the Historian, surrounded by its complex equipment, can date any object, carbon-based or otherwise, to within a decade of its origin, regardless of its state of preservation; and even the Moriteu is a thing of beauty and fascination as it gently separates the artifacts from the strata where they have rested for so long.

I am very glad I was chosen to come on this mission.

We have been here for two lunar cycles now, and the work goes slowly. The lower strata were thoroughly excavated eons ago (I have such a personal interest in learning about Man that I almost used the word *plundered* rather than *excavated*, so resentful am I at not finding more artifacts), and for reasons as yet unknown there is almost nothing in the more recent strata.

Most of us are pleased with our results, and Bellidore is particularly elated. He says that finding five nearly intact artifacts makes the expedition an unqualified success.

All the others have worked tirelessly since our arrival. Now it is almost time for me to perform my special function, and I am very excited. I know that my findings will be no more important that the others', but perhaps, when we put them all together, we can finally begin to understand what it was that made Man what he was.

"Are you..." asked the first Stardust Twin.

"...ready?" said the second.

I answered that I was ready, that indeed I had been anxious for this moment.

"May we..."

"...observe?" they asked.

"If you do not find it distasteful," I replied.

"We are...

"...scientists," they said. "There is..."

"...very little..."

"...that we cannot view..."

"...objectively."

I ambulated to the table upon which the artifact rested. It was a stone, or at least that is what it appeared to be to my exterior sensory organs. It was triangular, and the edges showed signs of work.

"How old is this?" I asked.

"Three million..."

"...five hundred and sixty-one thousand..."

"...eight hundred and twelve years," answered the Stardust Twins.

"I see," I said.

"It is much..."

"...the oldest..."

"...of our finds."

I stared at it for a long time, preparing myself. Then I slowly, carefully, altered my structure and allowed my body to flow over and around the stone, engulfing it, and assimilating its history. I began to feel a delicious warmth as it became one with me, and while all my exterior senses had shut down, I knew that I was undulating and glowing with the thrill of discovery. I became one with the stone, and in that corner of my mind that is set aside for Feeling, I seemed to sense the Earth's moon looming low and ominous just above the horizon...

★ ★ ★

Enkatai awoke with a start just after dawn and looked up at the moon, which was still high in the sky. After all these weeks it still seemed far too large to hang suspended in the sky, and must surely crash down onto the planet any moment. The nightmare was still strong in her mind, and she tried to imagine the comforting sight of five small, unthreatening moons leapfrogging across the silver sky of her own world. She was able to hold the vision in her mind's eye for only a moment, and then it was lost, replaced by the reality of the huge satellite above her.

Her companion approached her.

"Another dream?" he asked.

"Exactly like the last one," she said uncomfortably. "The moon is visible in the daylight, and then we begin walking down the path..."

He stared at her with sympathy and offered her nourishment. She accepted it gratefully, and looked off across the veldt.

"Just two more days," she sighed, "and then we can leave this awful place."

"It is not such a terrible world," replied Bokatu. "It has many good qualities."

"We have wasted our time here," she said. "It is not fit for colonization."

"No, it is not," he agreed. "Our crops cannot thrive in this soil, and we have problems with the water. But we have learned many things, things that will eventually help us choose the proper world."

"We learned most of them the first week we were here," said Enkatai. "The rest of the time was wasted."

"The ship had other worlds to explore. They could not know we would be able to analyze this one in such a short time."

She shivered in the cool morning air. "I hate this place."

"It will someday be a fine world," said Bokatu. "It awaits only the evolution of the brown monkeys."

Even as he spoke, an enormous baboon, some 350 pounds in weight, heavily muscled, with a shaggy chest and bold, curious eyes, appeared in the distance. Even walking on all fours it was a formidable figure, fully twice as large as the great spotted cats.

"*We* cannot use this world," continued Bokatu, "but someday *his* descendants will spread across it."

"They seem so placid," commented Enkatai.

"They *are* placid," agreed Bokatu, hurling a piece of food at the baboon, which raced forward and picked it up off the ground. It sniffed at it, seemed to consider whether or not to taste it, and finally, after a moment of indecision, put it in its mouth. "But they will dominate this planet. The huge grass-eaters spend too much time feeding, and the predators sleep all the time. No, my choice is the brown monkey. They are fine, strong, intelligent animals. They have already developed thumbs, they possess a strong sense of community, and even the great cats think twice about attacking them. They are virtually without natural predators." He nodded his head, agreeing with himself. "Yes, it is they who will dominate this world in the eons to come."

"No predators?" said Enkatai.

"Oh, I suppose one falls prey to the great cats now and then, but even the cats do not attack when they are with their troop." He looked at the baboon. "That fellow has the strength to tear all but the biggest cat to pieces."

"Then how do you account for what we found at the bottom of the gorge?" she persisted.

"Their size has cost them some degree of agility. It is only natural that one occasionally falls down the slopes to its death."

"Occasionally?" she repeated. "I found seven skulls, each shattered as if from a blow."

"The force of the fall," said Bokatu with a shrug. "Surely you don't think the great cats brained them before killing them?"

"I wasn't thinking of the cats," she replied.

"What, then?"

"The small, tailless monkeys that live in the gorge."

Bokatu allowed himself the luxury of a superior smile. "Have you *looked* at them?" he said. "They are scarcely a quarter the size of the brown monkeys."

"I *have* looked at them," answered Enkatai. "And they, too, have thumbs."

"Thumbs alone are not enough," said Bokatu.

"They live in the shadow of the brown monkeys, and they are still here," she said. "*That* is enough."

"The brown monkeys are eaters of fruits and leaves. Why should they bother the tailless monkeys?"

"They do more than not bother them," said Enkatai. "They avoid them. That hardly seems like a species that will someday spread across the world."

Bokatu shook his head. "The tailless monkeys seem to be at an evolutionary dead end. Too small to hunt game, too large to feed themselves on what they can find in the gorge, too weak to compete with the brown monkeys for better territory. My guess is that they're an earlier, more primitive species, destined for extinction."

"Perhaps," said Enkatai.

"You disagree?"

"There is something about them..."

"What?"

Enkatai shrugged. "I do not know. They make me uneasy. It is something in their eyes, I think—a hint of malevolence."

"You are imagining things," said Bokatu.

"Perhaps," replied Enkatai again.

"I have reports to write today," said Bokatu. "But tomorrow I will prove it to you."

The next morning Bokatu was up with the sun. He prepared their first meal of the day while Enkatai completed her prayers, then performed his own while she ate.

"Now," he announced, "we will go down into the gorge and capture one of the tailless monkeys."

"Why?"

"To show you how easy it is. I may take it back with me as a pet. Or perhaps we shall sacrifice it in the lab and learn more about its life processes."

"I do not *want* a pet, and we are not authorized to kill any animals."

"As you wish," said Bokatu. "We will let it go."

"Then why capture one to begin with?"

"To show you that they are not intelligent, for if they are as bright as you think, I will not be able to capture one." He pulled her to an upright position. "Let us begin."

"This is foolish," she protested. "The ship arrives in midafternoon. Why don't we just wait for it?"

"We will be back in time," he replied confidently. "How long can it take?"

She looked at the clear blue sky, as if trying to urge the ship to appear. The moon was hanging, huge and pale, just above the horizon. Finally she turned to him.

"All right, I will come with you—but only if you promise merely to observe them, and not to try to capture one."

"Then you admit I'm right?"

"Saying that you are right or wrong has nothing to do with the truth of the situation. I *hope* you are right, for the tailless monkeys frighten me. But I do not know you are right, and neither do you."

Bokatu stared at her for a long moment.

"I agree," he said at last.

"You agree that you cannot know?"

"I agree not to capture one," he said. "Let us proceed."

They walked to the edge of the gorge and then began climbing down the steep embankments, steadying themselves by wrapping their limbs around trees and other outgrowths. Suddenly they heard a loud screeching.

"What is that?" asked Bokatu.

"They have seen us," replied Enkatai.

"What makes you think so?"

"I have heard that scream in my dream—and always the moon was just as it appears now."

"Strange," mused Bokatu. "I have heard them many times before, but somehow they seem louder this time."

"Perhaps more of them are here."

"Or perhaps they are more frightened," he said. He glanced above him. "Here is the reason," he said, pointing. "We have company."

She looked up and saw a huge baboon, quite the largest she had yet seen, following them at a distance of perhaps fifty feet. When its eyes met hers it growled and looked away, but made no attempt to move any closer or farther away.

They kept climbing, and whenever they stopped to rest, there was the baboon, its accustomed fifty feet away from them.

"Does *he* look afraid to you?" asked Bokatu. "If these puny little creatures could harm him, would he be following us down into the gorge?"

"There is a thin line between courage and foolishness, and an even thinner line between confidence and over-confidence," replied Enkatai.

"If he is to die here, it will be like all the others," said Bokatu. "He will lose his footing and fall to his death."

"You do not find it unusual that every one of them fell on its head?" she asked mildly.

"They broke every bone in their bodies," he replied. "I don't know why you consider only the heads."

"Because you do not get identical head wounds from different incidents."

"You have an overactive imagination," said Bokatu. He pointed to a small hairy figure that was staring up at them. "Does *that* look like something that could kill our friend here?"

The baboon glared down into the gorge and snarled. The tailless monkey looked up with no show of fear or even interest. Finally it shuffled off into the thick bush.

"You see?" said Bokatu smugly. "One look at the brown monkey and it retreats out of sight."

"It didn't seem frightened to me," noted Enkatai.

"All the more reason to doubt its intelligence."

In another few minutes they reached the spot where the tailless monkey had been. They paused to regain their strength, and then continued to the floor of the gorge.

"Nothing," announced Bokatu, looking around. "My guess is that the one we saw was a sentry, and by now the whole tribe is miles away."

"Observe our companion."

The baboon had reached the floor of the gorge and was tensely testing the wind.

"He hasn't crossed over the evolutionary barrier yet," said Bokatu, amused. "Do you expect him to search for predators with a sensor?"

"No," said Enkatai, watching the baboon. "But if there is no danger, I expect him to relax, and he hasn't done that yet."

"That's probably how he lived long enough to grow this large," said Bokatu, dismissing her remarks. He looked around. "What could they possibly find to eat here?"

"I don't know."

"Perhaps we should capture one and dissect it. The contents of its stomach might tell us a lot about it."

"You promised."

"It would be so simple, though," he persisted. "All we'd have to do would be bait a trap with fruits or nuts."

Suddenly the baboon snarled, and Bokatu and Eknatai turned to locate the source of his anger. There was nothing there, but the baboon became more and more frenzied. Finally it raced back up the gorge.

"What was that all about, I wonder?" mused Bokatu.

"I think we should leave."

"We have half a day before the ship returns."

"I am uneasy here. I walked down a path exactly like this in my dream."

"You are not used to the sunlight," he said. "We will rest inside a cave."

She reluctantly allowed him to lead her to a small cave in the wall of the gorge. Suddenly she stopped and would go no further.

"What is the matter?"

"This cave was in my dream," she said. "Do not go into it."

"You must learn not to let dreams rule your life," said Bokatu. He sniffed the air. "Something smells strange."

"Let us go back. We want nothing to do with this place."

He stuck his head into the cave. "New world, new odors."

"Please, Bokatu!"

"Let me just see what causes that odor," he said, shining his light into the cave. It illuminated a huge pile of bodies, many of them half-eaten, most in various states of decomposition.

"What are they?" he asked, stepping closer.

"Brown monkeys," she replied without looking. "Each with its head staved in."

"This was part of your dream, too?" he asked, suddenly nervous.

She nodded her head. "We must leave this place *now*!"

He walked to the mouth of the cave.

"It seems safe," he announced.

"It is never safe in my dream," she said uneasily.

They left the cave and walked about fifty yards when they came to a bend in the floor of the gorge. As they followed it, they found themselves facing a tailless monkey.

"One of them seems to have stayed behind," said Bokatu. "I'll frighten him away." He picked up a rock and threw it at the monkey, which ducked but held its ground.

Enkatai touched him urgently on the shoulder. "More than one," she said.

He looked up. Two more tailless monkeys were in a tree almost directly overhead. As he stepped aside, he saw four more lumbering toward them out of the bush. Another emerged from a cave, and three more dropped out of nearby trees.

"What have they got in their hands?" he asked nervously.

"You would call them the femur bones of grass-eaters," said Enkatai, with a sick feeling in her thorax. "*They* would call them weapons."

The hairless monkeys spread out in a semi-circle, then began approaching them slowly.

"But they're so *puny*!" said Bokatu, backing up until he came to a wall of rock and could go no farther.

"You are a fool," said Enkatai, helplessly trapped in the reality of her dream. "*This* is the race that will dominate this planet. Look into their eyes!"

Bokatu looked, and he saw things, terrifying things, that he had never seen in any being or any animal before. He barely had time to offer a brief prayer for some disaster to befall this race before it could reach the stars, and then a tailless monkey hurled a smooth, polished, triangular stone at his head. It dazed him, and as he fell to the ground, the clubs began pounding down rhythmically on him and Enkatai.

At the top of the gorge, the baboon watched the carnage until it was over, and then raced off toward the vast savannah, where he would be safe, at least temporarily, from the tailless monkeys.

★ ★ ★

"A weapon," I mused. "It was a *weapon*!"

I was all alone. Sometime during the Feeling, the Stardust Twins had decided that I was one of the few things they could not be objective about, and had returned to their quarters.

I waited until the excitement of discovery had diminished enough for me to control my physical structure. Then I once again took the shape that I presented to my companions, and reported my findings to Bellidore.

"So even then they were aggressors," he said. "Well, it is not surprising. The will to dominate the stars had to have come from somewhere."

"It is surprising that there is no record of any race having landed here in their prehistory," said the Historian.

"It was a survey team, and Earth was of no use to them," I answered. "They doubtless touched down on any number of planets. If there is a record anywhere, it is probably in their archives, stating that Earth showed no promise as a colony world."

"But didn't they wonder what had happened to their team?" asked Bellidore.

"There were many large carnivores in the vicinity," I said. "They probably assumed the team had fallen prey to them. Especially if they searched the area and found nothing."

"Interesting," said Bellidore. "That the weaker of the species should have risen to dominance."

"I think it is easily explained," said the Historian. "*As* the smaller species, they were neither as fast as their prey nor as strong as their predators, so the creation of weapons was perhaps the only way to avoid extinction...or at least the best way."

"Certainly they displayed the cunning of the predator during their millennia abroad in the galaxy," said Bellidore.

"One does not *stop* being aggressive simply because one invents a weapon," said the Historian. "In fact, it may *add* to one's aggression."

"I shall have to consider that," said Bellidore, looking somewhat unconvinced.

"I have perhaps over-simplified my train of thought for the sake of this discussion," replied the Historian. "Rest assured that I will build a lengthy and rigorous argument when I present my findings to the Academy."

"And what of you, He Who Views?" asked Bellidore. "Have you any observations to add to what you have told us?"

"It is difficult to think of a rock as being the percursor of the sonic rifle and the molecular imploder," I said thoughtfully, "but I believe it to be the case."

"A most interesting species," said Bellidore.

It took almost four hours for my strength to return, for Feeling saps the energy like no other function, drawing equally from the body, the emotions, the mind, and the empathic powers.

The Moriteu, its work done for the day, was hanging upside down from a tree limb, lost in its evening trance, and the Stardust Twins had not made an appearance since I had Felt the stone.

The other party members were busy with their own pursuits, and it seemed an ideal time for me to Feel the next object, which the Historian told me was approximately 23,300 years old.

It was a link of metallic chain, rusted and pitted, and before I assimilated it, I thought I could see a spot where it had been deliberately broken...

★ ★ ★

His name was Mtepwa, and it seemed to him that he had been wearing a metal collar around his neck since the day he had been born. He knew that couldn't be true, for he had fleeting memories of playing with his brothers and sisters, and of stalking the kudu and the bongo on the tree-covered mountain where he grew up.

But the more he concentrated on those memories, the more vague and imprecise they became, and he knew they must have happened a very long time ago. Sometimes he tried to remember the name of his tribe, but it was lost in the mists of time, as were the names of his parents and siblings.

It was at times like this that Mtepwa felt sorry for himself, but then he would consider his companions' situation, and he felt better, for while they were to be taken in ships and sent to the edge of the world to spend the remainder of their lives as slaves of the Arabs and the Europeans, he himself was the favored servant of his master, Sharif Abdullah, and as such his position was assured.

This was his eighth caravan—or was it his ninth?—from the Interior. They would trade salt and cartridges to the tribal chiefs who would in turn sell them their least productive warriors and women as slaves, and then they would march them out, around the huge lake and across the dry flat savannah. They would circle the mountain that was so old that it had turned white on the top, just like a white-haired old man, and finally out to the coast, where dhows filled the harbor. There they would sell their human booty to the highest bidders, and Sharif Abdullah would purchase another wife and turn half the money over to his aged, feeble father, and they would be off to the Interior again on another quest for black gold.

Abdullah was a good master. He rarely drank—and when he did, he always apologized to Allah at the next opportunity—and he did not beat Mtepwa overly much, and they always had enough to eat, even when the cargo went hungry. He even went so far as to teach Mtepwa how to read, although the only reading matter he carried with him was the Koran.

Mtepwa spent long hours honing his reading skills with the Koran, and somewhere along the way he made a most interesting discovery: the Koran forbade a practitioner of the True Faith to keep another member in bondage.

It was at that moment that Mtepwa made up his mind to convert to Islam. He began questioning Sharif Abdullah incessantly on the finer points of his religion, and made sure that the old man saw him sitting by the fire, hour after hour, reading the Koran.

So enthused was Sharif Abdullah at this development that he frequently invited Mtepwa into his tent at suppertime, and lectured him on the subtleties of the Koran far into the night. Mtepwa was a motivated student, and Sharif Abdullah marveled at his enthusiasm.

Night after night, as lions prowled around their camp in the Serengeti, master and pupil studied the Koran together. And finally the day came when Sharif Abdullah could not longer deny that Mtepwa was indeed a true believer of Islam. It happened as they camped at the Olduvai Gorge, and that very day Sharif Abdullah had his smith remove the collar from Mtepwa's neck, and Mtepwa himself destroyed the chains link by link, hurling them deep into the gorge when he was finished. He kept a single link, which he wore suspended from his neck as a charm.

Mtepwa was now a free man, but knowledgable in only two areas: the Koran, and slave-trading. So it was only natural that when he looked around for some means to support himself, he settled upon following in Sharif Abdullah's footsteps. He became a junior partner to the old man, and after two more trips to the Interior, he decided that he was ready to go out on his own.

To do that, he required a trained staff—warriors, smiths, cooks, trackers—and the prospect of assembling one from scratch was daunting, so, since his faith was less strong than his mentor's, he simply sneaked into Sharif Abdullah's quarters on the coast one night and slit the old man's throat.

The next day, he marched inland at the head of his own caravan.

He had learned much about the business of slaving, both as a practitioner and a victim, and he put his knwoledge to full use. He knew that healthy slaves would bring a better price at market, and so he fed and treated his captives far better than Sharif Abdullah and most other slavers did. On the other hand, he knew which ones were fomenting trouble, and knew it was better to kill them on the spot as an example to the others, than to let any hopes of insurrection spread among the captives.

Because he was thorough, he was equally successful, and soon expanded into ivory trading as well. Within six years he had the biggest slaving and poaching operation in East Africa.

From time to time he ran across European explorers. It was said that he even spent a week with Dr. David Livingstone and left without the missionary ever knowing that he had been playing host to the slaver he most wanted to put out of business.

After America's War Between the States killed his primary market, he took a year off from his operation to go to Asia and the Arabian Peninsula and open up new ones. Upon returning he found that Abdullah's son, Sharif Ibn Jad Mahir, had appropriated all his men and headed inland, intent on carrying on his father's business. Mtepwa, who had become quite wealthy, hired some 500 *askari*, placed them under the command of the notorious ivory poacher Alfred Henry Pym, and sat back to await the results.

Three months later Pym marched some 438 men back to the Tanganyikan coast. 276 were slaves that Sharif Ibn Jad Mahir had captured; the remainder were the remnants of Mtepwa's organization, who had gone to work for Sharif Ibn Jad Mahir. Mtepwa sold all 438 of them into slavery and built a new organization, composed of the warriors who had fought for him under Pym's leadership.

Most of the colonial powers were inclined to turn a blind eye to his practices, but the British, who were determined to put an end to slavery, issued a warrant for Mtepwa's arrest. Eventually he tired of continually looking over his shoulder, and moved his headquarters to Mozambique, where the Portugese were happy to let him set up shop as long as he remembered that colonial palms needed constant greasing.

He was never happy there—he didn't speak Portugese or any of the local languages—and after nine years he returned to Tanganyika, now the wealthiest black man on the continent.

One day he found among his latest batch of captives a young Acholi boy named Haradi, no more than ten years old, and decided to keep him as a personal servant rather than ship him across the ocean.

Mtepwa had never married. Most of his associates assumed that he had simply never had the time, but as the almost-nightly demands for Haradi to visit him in his tent became common knowledge, they soon revised their opinions. Mtepwa seemed besotted with his servant boy, though—doubtless remembering his own experience—he never taught Haradi to read, and promised a slow and painful death to anyone who spoke of Islam to the boy.

Then one night, after some three years had passed, Mtepwa sent for Haradi. The boy was nowhere to be found. Mtepwa awoke all his warriors and demanded that they search for him, for a leopard had been seen in the vicinity of the camp, and the slaver feared the worst.

They found Haradi an hour later, not in the jaws of a leopard, but in the arms of a young female slave they had taken from the Zanake tribe. Mtepwa was beside himself with rage, and had the poor girl's arms and legs torn from her body.

Haradi never offered a word of protest, and never tried to defend the girl—not that it would have done any good—but the next morning he was gone, and though Mtepwa and his warriors spent almost a month searching for him, they found no trace of him.

By the end of the month Mtepwa was quite insane with rage and grief. Deciding that life was no longer worth living, he walked up to a pride of lions that were gorging themselves on a topi carcass and, striding into their midst, began cursing them and hitting them with his bare hands. Almost unbelievably, the lions backed away from him, snarling and growling, and disappeared into the thick bush.

The next day he picked up a large stick and began beating a baby elephant with it. That should have precipitated a brutal attack by its mother—but the mother, standing only a few feet away, trumpeted in terror and raced off, the baby following her as best it could.

It was then that Mtepwa decided that he could not die, that somehow the act of dismembering the poor Zanake girl had made him immortal. Since both incidents had occured within sight of his superstitious followers, they fervently believed him.

Now that he was immortal, he decided that it was time to stop trying to accomodate the Europeans who had invaded his land and kept issuing warrents for his arrest. He sent a runner to the Kenya border and invited the British to meet him in battle. When the appointed day came, and the British did not show up to fight him, he confidently told his warriors that word of his immortality had reached the Europeans and that from that day forth no white men would ever be willing to oppose him. The fact that he was still in German territory, and the British had no legal right to go there, somehow managed to elude him.

He began marching his warriors inland, openly in search of slaves, and he found his share of them in the Congo. He looted villages of their men, their women, and their ivory, and finally, with almost 600 captives and half that many tusks, he finally turned east and began the months-long trek to the coast.

This time the British were waiting for him at the Uganda border, and they had so many armed men there that Mtepwa turned south, not for fear for his own life, but because he could not afford to lose his slaves and his ivory, and he knew that his warriors lacked his invulnerability.

He marched his army down to Lake Tanganyika, then headed east. It took him two weeks to reach the western corridor of the Serengeti, and another ten days to cross it.

One night he made camp at the lip of the Olduvai Gorge, the very place where he had gained his freedom. The fires were lit, a wildebeest was slaughtered and cooked, and as he relaxed after the meal he became aware of a buzzing among his men. Then, from out of the shadows, stepped a strangely familiar figure. It was Haradi, now fifteen years old, and as tall as Mtepwa himself.

Mtepwa stared at him for a long moment, and suddenly all the anger seemed to drain from his face.

"I am very glad to see you again, Haradi," he said.

"I have heard that you cannot be killed," answered the boy, brandishing a spear. "I have come to see if that is true."

"We have no need to fight, you and I," said Mtepwa. "Join me in my tent, and all will be as it was."

"Once I tear your limbs from your body, *then* we will have no reason to fight," responded Haradi. "And even then, you will seem no less repulsive to me than you do now, or than you did all those many years ago."

Mtepwa jumped up, his face a mask of fury. "Do your worst, then!" he cried. "And when you realize that I cannot be harmed, I will do to you as I did to the Zanake girl!"

Haradi made no reply, but hurled his spear at Mtepwa. It went into the slaver's body, and was thrown with such force that the point emerged a good six inches on the other side. Mtepwa stared at Haradi with disbelief, moaned once, and tumbled down the rocky slopes of the gorge.

Haradi looked around at the warriors. "Is there any among you who dispute my right to take Mtepwa's place?" he asked confidently.

A burly Makonde stood up to challenge him, and within thirty seconds Haradi, too, was dead.

The British were waiting for them when they reached Zanzibar. The slaves were freed, the ivory confiscated, the warriors arrested and forced to serve as laborers on the Mombasa/Uganda Railway. Two of them were later killed and eaten by lions in the Tsavo District.

By the time Lieutenant-Colonel J. H. Patterson shot the notorious Man-Eaters of Tsavo, the railway had almost reached the shanty town of Nairobi, and Mtepwa's name was so thoroughly forgotten that it was misspelled in the only history book in which it appeared.

★ ★ ★

"Amazing!" said the Appraiser. "I knew they enslaved many races throughout the galaxy—but to enslave *themselves*! It is almost beyond belief!"

I had rested from my efforts, and then related the story of Mtepwa.

"All ideas must begin somewhere," said Bellidore placidly. "This one obviously began on Earth."

"It is barbaric!" muttered the Appraiser.

Bellidore turned to me. "Man never attempted to subjugate *your* race, He Who Views. Why was that?"

"We had nothing that he wanted."

"Can you remember the galaxy when Man dominated it?" asked the Appraiser.

"I can remember the galaxy when Man's progenitors killed Bokatu and Enkatai," I replied truthfully.

"Did you ever have any dealings with Man?"

"None. Man had no use for us."

"But did he not destroy profligately things for which he had no use?"

"No," I said. "He took what he wanted, and he destroyed that which threatened him. The rest he ignored."

"Such arrogance!"

"Such practicality," said Bellidore.

"You call genocide on a galactic scale *practical*?" demanded the Appraiser.

"From Man's point of view, it was," answered Bellidore. "It got him what he wanted with a minimum of risk and effort. Consider that one single race, born not five hundred yards from us, at one time ruled an empire of more than a million worlds. Almost every civilized race in the galaxy spoke Terran."

"Upon pain of death."

"That is true," agreed Bellidore. "I did not say Man was an angel. Only that if he was indeed a devil, he was an efficient one."

It was time for me to assimilate the third artifact, which the Historian and the Appraiser seemed to think was the handle of a knife, but even as I moved off to perform my function, I could not help but listen to the speculation that was taking place.

"Given his bloodlust and his efficiency," said the Appraiser, "I'm surprised that he lived long enough to reach the stars."

"It *is* surprising in a way," agreed Bellidore. "The Historian tells me that Man was not always homogenous, that early in his history there were several variations of the species. He was divided by color, by belief, by territory." He sighed. "Still, he must have learned to live in peace with his fellow man. That much, at least, accrues to his credit."

I reached the artifact with Bellidore's words still in my ears, and began to engulf it...

* * *

Mary Leakey pressed against the horn of the Landrover. Inside the museum, her husband turned to the young uniformed officer.

"I can't think of any instructions to give you," he said. "The museum's not open to the public yet, and we're a good 300 kilometers from Kikuyuland."

"I'm just following my orders, Dr. Leakey," replied the officer.

"Well, I suppose it doesn't hurt to be safe," acknowledged Leakey. "There are a lot of Kikuyu who want me dead even though I spoke up for Kenyatta at his trial." He walked to the door. "If the discoveries at Lake Turkana prove interesting, we could be gone as long as a month. Otherwise, we should be back within ten to twelve days."

"No problem, sir. The museum will still be here when you get back."

"I never doubted it," said Leakey, walking out and joining his wife in the vehicle.

Lieutenant Ian Chelmswood stood in the doorway and watched the Leakeys, accompanied by two military vehicles, start down the red dirt road. Within seconds the car was obscured by dust, and he stepped back into the building and closed the door to avoid being covered by it. The heat was oppressive, and he removed his jacket and holster and laid them neatly across one of the small display cases.

It was strange. All the images he had seen of African wildlife, from the German Schillings' old still photographs to the American Johnson's motion pictures, had led him to believe that East Africa was a wonderland of green grass and clear water. No one had ever mentioned the dust, but that was the one memory of it that he would take home with him.

Well, not quite the only one. He would never forget the morning the alarm had sounded back when he was stationed in Nanyuki. He arrived at the settlers' farm and found the entire family cut to ribbons and all their cattle mutilated, most with their genitals cut off, many missing ears and eyes. But as horrible as that was, the picture he would carry to his grave was the kitten impaled on a dagger and pinned to the mailbox. It was the Mau Mau's signature, just in case anyone thought some madman had run beserk among the cattle and the humans.

Chelmswood didn't understand the politics of it. He didn't know who had started it, who had precipitated the war. It made no difference to him. He was just a soldier, following orders, and if those orders would take him back to Nanyuki so that he could kill the men who had committed those atrocities, so much the better.

But in the meantime, he had pulled what he considered Idiot Duty. There had been a very mild outburst of violence in Arusha, not really Mau Mau but rather a show of support for Kenya's Kikuyu, and his unit had been transferred there. Then the government found out that Professor Leakey, whose scientific finds had made Olduvai Gorge almost a household word among East Africans, had been getting death threats. Over his objections, they had insisted on providing him with bodyguards. Most of the men from Chelmswood's unit would accompany Leakey on his trip to Lake Turkana, but someone had to stay behind to guard the museum, and it was just his bad luck that his name had been atop the duty roster.

It wasn't even a museum, really, not the kind of museum his parents had taken him to see in London. *Those* were museums; this was just a two-room mud-walled structure with perhaps a hundred of Leakey's finds. Ancient arrowheads, some oddly-shaped stones that had functioned as prehistoric tools, a couple of bones that obviously weren't from monkeys but that Chelmswood was certain were not from any creature *he* was related to.

Leakey had hung some crudely-drawn charts on the wall, charts that showed what he believed to be the evolution of some small, grotesque, apelike beasts into *homo sapiens.* There were photographs, too, showing some of the finds that had been sent on to Nairobi. It seemed that even if this gorge was the birthplace of the race, nobody really wanted to visit it. All the best finds were shipped back to Nairobi and then to the British Museum. In fact, this wasn't a museum at all, decided Chelmswood, but rather a holding area for the better specimens until they could be sent elsewhere.

It was strange to think of life starting here in this gorge. If there was an uglier spot in Africa, he had yet to come across it. And while he didn't accept Genesis or any of that religious nonsense, it bothered him to think that the first human beings to walk the Earth might have been black. He'd hardly had any exposure to blacks when he was growing up in the Cotswolds, but he'd seen enough of what they could do since coming to British East, and he was apalled by their savagery and barbarism.

And what about those crazy Americans, wringing their hands and saying that colonialism had to end? If they had seen what *he'd* seen on that farm in Nanyuki, they'd know that the only thing that was keeping all of East Africa from exploding into an unholy conflagration of blood and butchery was the British presence. Certainly, there were parallels between the Mau Mau and America: both had been colonized by the British and both wanted their independence...but there all similarity ended. The Americans wrote a Declaration outlining their grievances, and then they fielded an army and fought the British *soldiers.* What did chopping up innocent children and pinning cats to mailboxes have in common with that? If he had his way, he'd march in half a million British troops, wipe out every last Kikuyu—except for the good ones, the loyal ones—and solve the problem once and for all.

He wandered over to the cabinet where Leakey kept his beer and pulled out a warm bottle. Safari brand. He opened it and took a long swallow, then made a face. If that's what people drank on safari, he'd have to remember never to go on one.

And yet he knew that someday he *would* go on safari, hopefully before he was mustered out and sent home. Parts of the country were so damned beautiful, dust or no dust, and he liked the thought of sitting beneath a shade tree, cold drink in hand, while his body servant cooled him with a fan made of ostrich feathers and he and his white hunter discussed the day's kills and what they would go out after tomorrow. It wasn't the shooting that was important, they'd both reassure themselves, but rather the thrill of the hunt. Then he'd have a couple of his black boys draw his bath, and he'd bathe and prepare for dinner. Funny how he had fallen into the habit of calling them boys; most of them were far older than he.

But while they weren't boys, they *were* children in need of guidance and civilizing. Take those Maasai, for example; proud, arrogant bastards. They looked great on postcards, but try *dealing* with them. They acted as if they had a direct line to God, that He had told them they were His chosen people. The more Chelmswood thought about it, the more surprised he was that it was the Kikuyu that had begun Mau Mau rather than the Maasai. And come to think of it, he'd notice four or five Maasai *elmorani* hanging around the museum. He'd have to keep an eye on them...

"Excuse, please?" said a high-pitched voice, and Chelmswood turned to see a small skinny black boy, no more than ten years old, standing in the doorway.

"What do you want?" he asked.

"Doctor Mister Leakey, he promise me candy," said the boy, stepping inside the building.

"Go away," said Chelmswood irritably. "We don't have any candy here."

"Yes yes," said the boy, stepping forward. "Every day."

"He gives you candy every day?"

The boy nodded his head and smiled.

"Where does he keep it?"

The boy shrugged. "Maybe in there?" he said, pointing to a cabinet.

Chelmswood walked to the cabinet and opened it. There was nothing in it but four jars containing primitive teeth.

"I don't see any," he said. "You'll have to wait until Dr. Leakey comes back."

Two tears trickled down the boy's cheek. "But Doctor Mister Leakey, he *promise*!"

Chelmswood looked around. "I don't know where it is."

The boy began crying in earnest.

"Be quiet!" snapped Chelmswood. "I'll look for it."

"Maybe next room," suggested the boy.

"Come along," said Chelmswood, walking through the doorway to the adjoining room. He looked around, hands on hips, trying to imagine where Leakey had hidden the candy.

"This place maybe," said the boy, pointing to a closet.

Chelmswood opened the closet. It contained two spades, three picks, and an assortment of small brushes, all of which he assumed were used by the Leakeys for their work.

"Nothing here," he said, closing the door.

He turned to face the boy, but found the room empty.

"Little bugger was lying all along," he muttered. "Probably ran away to save himself a beating."

He walked back into the main room—and found himself facing a well-built black man holding a machete-like *panga* in his right hand.

"What's going on here?" snapped Chelmswood.

"Freedom is going on here, Lieutenant," said the black man in near-perfect English. "I was sent to kill Dr. Leakey, but you will have to do."

"Why are you killing anyone?" demanded Chelmswood. "What did we ever do to the Maasai?"

"I will let the Maasai answer that. Any one of them could take one look at me and tell you than I am Kikuyu—but we are all the same to you British, aren't we?"

Chelmswood reached for his gun and suddenly realized he had left it on a display case.

"You all look like cowardly savages to me!"

"Why? Because we do not meet you in battle?" The black man's face filled with fury. "You take our land away, you forbid us to own weapons, you even make it a crime for us to carry spears— and then you call us savages when we don't march in formation against your guns!" He spat contemptuously on the floor. "We fight you in the only way that is left to us."

"It's a big country, big enough for both races," said Chelmswood.

"If we came to England and took away your best farmland and forced you to work for us, would you think England was big enough for both races?"

"I'm not political," said Chelmswood, edging another step closer to his weapon. "I'm just doing my job."

"And your job is to keep two hundred whites on land that once held a million Kikuyu," said the black man, his face reflecting his hatred.

"There'll be a lot less than a million when *we* get through with you!" hissed Chelmswood, diving for his gun.

Quick as he was, the black man was faster, and with a single swipe of his *panga* he almost severed the Englishman's right hand from his wrist.

Chelmswood bellowed in pain, and spun around, presenting his back to the Kikuyu as he reached for the pistol with his other hand.

The *panga* came down again, practically splitting him open, but as he fell he managed to get his fingers around the handle of his pistol and pull the trigger. The bullet struck the black man in the chest, and he, too, collapsed to the floor.

"You've killed me!" moaned Chelmswood. "Why would anyone want to kill me?"

"You have so much and we have so little," whispered the black man. "Why must you have what is ours, too?"

"What did I ever do to you?" asked Chelmswood.

"You came here. That was enough," said the black man. "Filthy English!" He closed his eyes and lay still.

"Bloody nigger!" slurred Chelmswood, and died.

Outside, the four Maasai paid no attention to the tumult within. They let the small Kikuyu boy leave without giving him so much as a glance. The business of inferior races was none of their concern.

★ ★ ★

"These notions of superiority among members of the same race are very difficult to comprehend," said Bellidore. "Are you *sure* you read the artifact properly, He Who Views?"

"I do not *read* artifacts," I replied. "I *assimilate* them. I become one with them. Everything *they* have experienced, *I* experience." I paused. "There can be no mistake."

"Well, it is difficult to fathom, especially in a species that would one day control most of the galaxy. Did they think *every* race they met was inferior to them?"

"They certainly behaved as if they did," said the Historian. "They seemed to respect only those races that stood up to them— and even then they felt that militarily defeating them was proof of their superiority."

"And yet we know from ancient records that primitive man worshipped non-sentient animals," put in the Exobiologist.

"They must not have been survived for any great length of time," suggested the Historian. "If Man treated the races of the galaxy with contempt, how much worse must he have treated the poor creatures with whom he shared his home world?"

"Perhaps he viewed them much the same as he viewed my own race," I offered. "If they had nothing he wanted, if they presented no threat..."

"They would have had something he wanted," said the Exobiologist. "He was a predator. They would have had meat."

"And land," added the Historian. "If even the galaxy was not enough to quench Man's thirst for territory, think how unwilling he would have been to share his own world."

"It is a question I suspect will never be answered," said Bellidore.

"Unless the answer lies in one of the remaining artifacts," agreed the Exobiologist.

I'm sure the remark was not meant to jar me from my lethargy, but it occurred to me that it had been half a day since I had assimilated the knife handle, and I had regained enough of my strength to examine the next artifact.

It was a metal stylus...

★ ★ ★

*February 15, 2103:*

*Well, we finally got here! The Supermole got us through the tunnel from New York to London in just over four hours. Even so we were twenty minutes late, missed our connection, and had to wait another five hours for the next flight to Khartoum. From there our means of transport got increasingly more primitive—jet planes to Nairobi and Arusha—and then a quick shuttle to our campsite, but we've finally put civilization behind us. I've never seen open spaces like this before; you're barely aware of the skyscrapers of Nyerere, the closest town.*

*After an orientation speech telling us what to expect and how to behave on safari, we got the afternoon off to meet our traveling companions. I'm the youngest member of the group: a trip like this just costs too much for most people my age to afford. Of course, most people my age don't have an Uncle Reuben who dies and leaves them a ton of money. (Well, it's probably about eight ounces of money, now that the safari is paid for. Ha ha.)*

*The lodge is quite rustic. They have quaint microwaves for warming our food, although most of us will be eating at the restaurants. I understand the Japanese and Brazilian ones are the most popular, the former for the food—real fish—and the latter for the entertainment. My roommate is Mr. Shiboni, an elderly Japanese gentleman who tells me he has been saving his money for fifteen years to come on this safari. He seems pleasant and good-natured; I hope he can survive the rigors of the trip.*

*I had really wanted a shower, just to get in the spirit of things, but water is scarce here, and it looks like I'll have to settle for the same old chemical dryshower. I know, I know, it disinfects as well as cleanses, but if I wanted all the comforts of home, I'd have stayed home and saved $150,000.*

*February 16:*

*We met our guide today. I don't know why, but he doesn't quite fit my preconception of an African safari guide. I was expecting some grizzled old veteran who had a wealth of stories to tell, who had maybe even seen a civet cat or a duiker before they became extinct. What we got was Kevin Ole Tambake, a young Maasai who can't be 25 years old and dresses in a suit while we all wear our khakis. Still, he's lived here all his life, so I suppose he knows his way around.*

*And I'll give him this: he's a wonderful storyteller. He spent half an hour telling us myths about how his people used to live in huts called manyattas, and how their rite of passage to manhood was to kill a lion with a spear. As if the government would let anyone kill an animal!*

*We spent the morning driving down into the Ngorongoro Crater. It's a collapsed caldara, or volcano, that was once taller than Kilimanjaro itself. Kevin says it used to teem with game, though I can't see how, since any game standing atop it when it collapsed would have been instantly killed.*

*I think the real reason we went there was just to get the kinks out of our safari vehicle and learn the proper protocol. Probably just as well. The air-conditioning wasn't working right in two of the compartments, the service mechanism couldn't get the temperature right on the iced drinks, and once, when we thought we saw a bird, three of us buzzed Kevin at the same time and jammed his communication line.*

*In the afternoon we went out to Serengeti. Kevin says it used to extend all the way to the Kenya border, but now it's just a 20-square-mile park adjacent to the Crater. About an hour into the game run we saw a ground squirrel, but he disappeared into a hole before I could adjust my holo camera. Still, he was very impressive. Varying shares of brown, with dark eyes and a fluffy tail. Kevin estimated that he went almost three pounds, and says he hasn't seen one that big since he was a boy.*

*Just before we returned to camp, Kevin got word on the radio from another driver that they had spotted two starlings nesting in a tree about eight miles north and east of us. The vehicle's computer told us we wouldn't be able to reach it before dark, so Kevin had it lock the spot in its memory and promised us that we'd go there first thing in the morning.*

*I opted for the Brazilian restaurant, and spent a few pleasant hours listening to the live band. A very nice end to the first full day of safari.*

*February 17:*

*We left at dawn in search of the starlings, and though we found the tree where they had been spotted, we never did see them. One of the passengers—I think it was the little man from Burma, though I'm not sure—must have complained, because Kevin soon announced to the entire party that this was a safari, that there was no guarantee of seeing any particular bird or animal, and that while he would do his best for us, one could never be certain where the game might be.*

*And then, just as he was talking, a banded mongoose almost a foot long appeared out of nowhere. It seemed to pay no attention to us, and Kevin announced that we were killing the motor and going into hover mode so the noise wouldn't scare it away.*

*After a minute or two everyone on the right side of the vehicle had gotten their holographs, and we slowly spun on our axis so that the left side could see him—but the movement must have scared him off, because though the maneuver took less than thirty seconds, he was nowhere to be seen when we came to rest again.*

*Kevin announced that the vehicle had captured the mongoose on its automated holos, and copies would be made available to anyone who had missed their holo opportunity.*

*We were feeling great—the right side of the vehicle, anyway—when we stopped for lunch, and during our afternoon game run we saw three yellow weaver birds building their spherical nests in a tree. Kevin let us out, warning us not to approach closer than thirty yards, and we spent almost an hour watching and holographing them.*

*All in all, a very satisfying day.*

*February 18:*

*Today we left camp about an hour after sunrise, and went to a new location: Olduvai Gorge.*

*Kevin announced that we would spend our last two days here, that with the encroachment of the cities and farms on all the flat land, the remaining big game was pretty much confined to the gulleys and slopes of the gorge.*

*No vehicle, not even our specially-equipped one, was capable of navigating its way through the gorge, so we all got out and began walking in single file behind Kevin.*

*Most of us found it very difficult to keep up with Kevin. He clambered up and down the rocks as if he'd been doing it all his life, whereas I can't remember the last time*

*I saw a stair that didn't move when I stood on it. We had trekked for perhaps half an hour when I heard one of the men at the back of our strung-out party give a cry and point to a spot at the bottom of the gorge, and we all looked and saw something racing away at phenomenal speed.*

*"Another squirrel?" I asked.*

*Kevin just smiled.*

*The man behind me said he thought it was a mongoose.*

*"What you saw," said Kevin, "was a dik-dik, the last surviving African antelope."*

*"How big was it?" asked a woman.*

*"About average size," said Kevin. "Perhaps ten inches at the shoulder."*

*Imagine anything ten inches high being called average!*

*Kevin explained that dik-diks were very territorial, and that this one wouldn't stray far from his home area. Which meant that if we were patient and quiet—and lucky—we'd be able to spot him again.*

*I asked Kevin how many dik-diks lived in the gorge, and he scratched his head and considered it for a moment and then guessed that there might be as many as ten. (And Yellowstone has only nineteen rabbits left! Is it any wonder that all the serious animal buffs come to Africa?)*

*We kept walking for another hour, and then broke for lunch, while Kevin gave us the history of the place, telling us all about Dr. Leakey's finds. There were probably still more skeletons to be dug up, he guessed, but the government didn't want to frighten any animals away from what had become their last refuge, so the bones would have to wait for some future generation to unearth them. Roughly translated, that meant that Tanzania wasn't going to give up the revenues from 300 tourists a week and turn over the crown jewel in their park system to a bunch of anthropologists. I can't say that I blame them.*

*Other parties had begun pouring into the gorge, and I think the entire safari population must have totaled almost 70 by the time lunch was over. The guides each seemed to have "their" areas marked out, and I noticed that rarely did we get within a quarter mile of any other parties.*

*Kevin asked us if we wanted to sit in the shade until the heat of the day had passed, but since this was our next-to-last day on safari we voted overwhelmingly to proceed as soon as we were through eating.*

*It couldn't have been ten minutes later that the disaster occurred. We were clambering down a steep slope in single file, Kevin in the lead as usual, and me right behind him, when I heard a grunt and then a surprised yell, and I looked back to see Mr. Shiboni tumbling down the path. Evidently he'd lost his footing, and we could hear the bones in his leg snap as he hurtled toward us.*

*Kevin positioned himself to stop him, and almost got knocked down the gorge himself before he finally stopped poor Mr. Shiboni. Then he knelt down next to the old gentleman to tend to his broken leg—but as he did so his keen eyes spotted something we all had missed, and suddenly he was bounding up the slopes like a monkey. He stopped where Mr. Shiboni had initially stumbled, squatted down, and examined something. Then, looking like Death itself, he picked up the object and brought it back down the path.*

*It was a dead lizard, fully-grown, almost eight inches long, and smashed flat by Mr. Shiboni. It was impossible to say whether his fall was caused by stepping on it, or whether it simply couldn't get out of the way once he began tumbling...but it made no difference: he was responsible for the death of an animal in a National Park.*

*I tried to remember the release we had signed, giving the Park System permission to instantly withdraw money from our accounts should we destroy an animal for any reason, even self-protection. I knew that the absolute minimum penalty was $50,000, but I think that was for two of the more common birds, and that ugaama and gecko lizards were in the $70,000 range.*

*Kevin held the lizard up for all of us to see, and told us that should legal action ensue, we were all witnesses to what had happened.*

*Mr. Shiboni groaned in pain, and Kevin said that there was no sense wasting the lizard, so he gave it to me to hold while he splinted Mr. Shiboni's leg and summoned the paramedics on the radio.*

*I began examining the little lizard. Its feet were finely-shaped, its tail long and elegant, but it was the colors that made the most lasting impression on me: a reddish head, a blue body, and grey legs, the color growing lighter as it reached the claws. A beautiful, beautiful thing, even in death.*

*After the paramedics had taken Mr. Shiboni back to the lodge, Kevin spent the next hour showing us how the ugaama lizard functioned: how its eyes could see in two directions as once, how its claws allowed it to hang upside down from any uneven surface, and how efficiently its jaws could crack the carapaces of the insects it caught. Finally, in view of the tragedy, and also because he wanted to check on Mr. Shiboni's condition, Kevin suggested that we call it a day.*

*None of us objected—we knew Kevin would have hours of extra work, writing up the incident and convincing the Park Department that his safari company was not responsible for it— but still we felt cheated, since there was only one day left. I think Kevin knew it, because just before we reached the lodge he promised us a special treat tomorrow.*

*I've been awake half the night wondering what it could be? Can he possibly know where the other dik-diks are? Or could the legends of a last flamingo possibly be true?*

*February 19:*

*We were all excited when we climbed aboard the vehicle this morning. Everyone kept asking Kevin what his "special treat" was, but he merely smiled and kept changing the subject. Finally we reached Olduvai Gorge and began walking, only this time we seemed to be going to a specific location, and Kevin hardly stopped to try to spot the dik-dik.*

*We climbed down twisting, winding paths, tripping over tree roots, cutting our arms and legs on thorn bushes, but nobody objected, for Kevin seemed so confident of his surprise that all these hardships were forgotten.*

*Finally we reached the bottom of the gorge and began walking along a flat winding path. Still, by the time we were ready to stop for lunch, we hadn't seen a thing. As we sat beneath the shade of an acacia tree, eating, Kevin pulled out his radio and conversed with the other guides. One group had seen three dik-diks, and another had found a lilac-breasted roller's nest with two hatchlings in it. Kevin is very competitive, and ordinarily news like that would have had him urging everyone to finish eating quickly so that we would not return to the lodge having seen less than everyone else, but this time he just smiled and told the other guides that we had seen nothing on the floor of the gorge and that the game seemed to have moved out, perhaps in search of water.*

*Then, when lunch was over, Kevin walked about 50 yards away, disappeared into a cave, and emerged a moment later with a small wooden cage. There was a little brown bird in it, and while I was thrilled to be able to see it close up, I felt somehow disappointed that this was to be the special treat.*

*"Have you ever seen a honey guide?" he asked.*

*We all admitted that we hadn't, and he explained that that was the name of the small brown bird.*

*I asked why it was called that, since it obviously didn't produce honey, and seemed incapable of replacing Kevin as our guide, and he smiled again.*

*"Do you see that tree?" he asked, pointing to a tree perhaps 75 yards away. There was a huge beehive on a low-hanging branch.*

*"Yes," I said.*

*"Then watch," he said, opening the cage and releasing the bird. It stood still for a moment, then fluttered its wings and took off in the direction of the tree.*

*"He is making sure there is honey there," explained Kevin, pointing to the bird as it circled the hive.*

*"Where is he going now?" I asked, as the bird suddenly flew down the river bed.*

*"To find his partner."*

*"Partner?" I asked, confused.*

*"Wait and see," said Kevin, sitting down with his back propped against a large rock.*

*We all followed suit and sat in the shade, our binoculars and holo cameras trained on the tree. After almost an hour nothing had happened, and some of us were getting restless, when Kevin tensed and pointed up the river bed.*

*"There!" he whispered.*

*I looked in the direction he was pointing, and there, following the bird, which was flying just ahead of him and chirping frantically, was an enormous black-and-white animal, the largest I have ever seen.*

*"What is it?" I whispered.*

*"A honey badger," answered Kevin softly. "They were thought to be extinct twenty years ago, but a mated pair took sanctuary in Olduvai. This is the fourth generation to be born here."*

*"Is he going to eat the bird?" asked one of the party.*

*"No," whispered Kevin. "The bird will lead him to the honey, and after he has pulled down the nest and eaten his fill, he will leave some for the bird."*

*And it was just as Kevin said. The honey badger climbed the bole of the tree and knocked off the beehive with a forepaw, then climbed back down and broke it apart, oblivious to the stings of the bees. We caught the whole fantastic scene on our holos, and when he was done he did indeed leave some honey for the honey guide.*

*Later, while Kevin was recapturing the bird and putting it back in its cage, the rest of us discussed what we had seen. I thought the honey badger must have weighed 45 pounds, though less excitable members of the party put its weight at closer to 36 or 37. Whichever it was, the creature was enormous. The discussion then shifted to how big a tip to leave for Kevin, for he had certainly earned one.*

*As I write this final entry in my safari diary, I am still trembling with the excitement that can only come from encountering big game in the wild. Prior to this afternoon, I had some doubts about the safari—I felt it was overpriced, or that perhaps my expectations had been too high—but now I know that it was worth every penny, and I have a feeling that I am leaving some part of me behind here, and that I will never be truly content until I return to this last bastion of the wilderness.*

★ ★ ★

The camp was abuzz with excitement. Just when we were sure that there were no more treasures to unearth, the Stardust Twins had found three small pieces of bone, attached together with a wire—obviously a human artifact.

"But the dates are wrong," said the Historian, after examining the bones thoroughly with its equipment. "This is a primitive piece of jewelry—for the adornment of savages, one might say—and yet the bones and wire both date from centuries after Man discovered space travel."

"Do you..."

"...deny that we..."

"...found it in the..."

...gorge?" demanded the Twins.

"I believe you," said the Historian. "I simply state that it seems to be an anachronism."

"It is our find, and..."

"...it will bear our name."

"No one is denying your right of discovery," said Bellidore. "It is simply that you have presented us with a mystery."

"Give it to..."

"...He Who Views, and he..."

"...will solve the mystery."

"I will do my best," I said. "But it has not been long enough since I assimilated the stylus. I must rest and regain my strength."

"That is..."

"...acceptable."

We let the Moriteu go about brushing and cleaning the artifact, while we speculated on why a primitive fetish should exist in the starfaring age. Finally the Exobiologist got to her feet.

"I am going back into the gorge," she announced. "If the Stardust Twins could find this, perhaps there are other things we have overlooked. After all, it is an enormous area." She paused and looked at the rest of us. "Would anyone care to come with me?"

It was nearing the end of the day, and no one volunteered, and finally the Exobiologist turned and began walking toward the path that led down into the depths of Olduvai Gorge.

It was dark when I finally felt strong enough to assimilate the jewelry. I spread my essence about the bones and the wire and soon became one with them...

★ ★ ★

His name was Joseph Meromo, and he could live with the money but not the guilt.

It had begun with the communication from Brussels, and the veiled suggestion from the head of the multi-national conglomerate headquartered there. They had a certain commodity to get rid of. They had no place to get rid of it. Could Tanzania help?

Meromo had told them he would look into it, but he doubted that his government could be of use.

Just *try*, came the reply.

In fact, more than the reply came. The next day a private courier delivered a huge wad of large-denomination bills, with a polite note thanking Meromo for his efforts on their behalf.

Meromo knew a bribe when he saw one—he'd certainly taken enough in his career—but he'd never seen one remotely the size of this one. And not even for helping them, but merely for being willing to explore possibilities.

Well, he had thought, why not? What could they conceivably have? A couple of containers of toxic waste? A few plutonium rods? You bury them deep enough in the earth and no one would ever know or care. Wasn't that what the Western countries did?

Of course, there was the Denver Disaster, and that little accident that made the Thames undrinkable for almost a century, but the only reason they popped so quickly to mind is because they were the *exceptions*, not the rule. There were thousands of dumping sites around the world, and 99% of them caused no problems at all.

Meromo had his computer cast a holographic map of Tanzania above his desk. He looked at it, frowned, added topographical features, then began studying it in earnest.

*If* he decided to help them dump the stuff, whatever it was —and he told himself that he was still uncommitted—where would be the best place to dispose of it?

Off the coast? No, the fishermen would pull it up two minutes later, take it to the press, and raise enough hell to get him fired, and possibly even cause the rest of the government to resign. The party really couldn't handle any more scandals this year.

The Selous Province? Maybe five centuries ago, when it was the last wilderness on the continent, but not now, not with a thriving, semi-autonomous city-state of fifty-two million people where once there had been nothing but elephants and almost-impenetrable thorn bush.

Lake Victoria? No. Same problem with the fishermen.

Dar es Salaam? It was a possibility. Close enough to the coast to make transport easy, practically deserted since Dodoma had become the new capital of the country.

But Dar es Salaam had been hit by an earthquake twenty years ago, when Meromo was still a boy, and he couldn't take the chance of another one exposing or breaking open whatever it was that he planned to hide.

He continued going over the map: Gombe, Ruaha, Iringa, Mbeya, Mtwara, Tarengire, Olduvai...

He stopped and stared at Olduvai, then called up all available data.

Almost a mile deep. That was in its favor. No animals left. Better still. No settlements on its steep slopes. Only a handful of Maasai still living in the area, no more than two dozen families, and they were too arrogant to pay any attention to what the government was doing. Of that Meromo was sure: he himself was a Maasai.

So he strung it out for as long as he could, collected cash gifts for almost two years, and finally gave them a delivery date.

Meromo stared out the window of his 34th floor office, past the bustling city of Dodoma, off to the east, to where he imagined Olduvai Gorge was.

It had seemed so simple. Yes, he was paid a lot of money, a disproportionate amount—but these multi-nationals had money to burn. It was just supposed to be a few dozen plutonium rods, or so he had thought. How was he to know that they were speaking of forty-two *tons* of nuclear waste?

There was no returning the money. Even if he wanted to, he could hardly expect them to come back and pull all that deadly material back out of the ground. Probably it was safe, probably no one would ever know...

But it haunted his days, and even worse, it began haunting his nights as well, appearing in various guises in his dreams. Sometimes it was as carefully-sealed containers, sometimes it was as ticking bombs, sometimes a disaster had already occurred and all he could see were the charred bodies of Maasai children spread across the lip of the gorge.

For almost eight months he fought his devils alone, but eventually he realized that he must have help. The dreams not only haunted him at night, but invaded the day as well. He would be sitting at a staff meeting, and suddenly he would imagine he was sitting among the emaciated, sore-covered bodies of the Olduvai Maasai. He would be reading a book, and the words seemed to change and he would be reading that Joseph Meromo had been sentenced to death for his greed. He would watch a holo of the Titanic disaster, and suddenly he was viewing some variation of the Olduvai Disaster.

Finally he went to a psychiatrist, and because he was a Maasai, he choose a Maasai psychiatrist. Fearing the doctor's contempt, Meromo would not state explicitly what was causing the nightmares and intrusions, and after almost half a year's worth of futile attempts to cure him, the psychiatrist announced that he could do no more.

"Then am I to be cursed with these dreams forever?" asked Meromo.

"Perhaps not," said the psychiatrist. "*I* cannot help you, but just possibly there is one man who can."

He rummaged through his desk and came up with a small white card. On it was written a single word: MULEWO.

"This is his business card," said the psychiatrist. "Take it."

"There is no address on it, no means of communicating with him," said Meromo. "How will I contact him?"

"He will contact you."

"You will give him my name?"

The psychiatrist shook his head. "I will not have to. Just keep the card on your person. He will know you require his services."

Meromo felt like he was being made the butt of some joke he didn't understand, but he dutifully put the card in his pocket and soon forgot about it.

Two weeks later, as he was drinking at a bar, putting off going home to sleep as long as he could, a small woman approached him.

"Are you Joseph Meromo?" she asked.

"Yes."

"Please follow me."

"Why?" he asked suspiciously.

"You have business with Mulewo, do you not?" she said.

Meromo fell into step behind her, at least as much to avoid going home as from any belief that this mysterious man with no first name could help him. They went out to the street, turned left, walked in silence for three blocks, and turned right, coming to a halt at the front door to a steel-and-glass skyscraper.

"The 63rd floor," she said. "He is expecting you."

"You're not coming with me?" asked Meromo.

She shook her head. "My job is done." She turned and walked off into the night.

Meromo looked up at the top of the building. It seemed residential. He considered his options, finally shrugged, and walk into the lobby.

"You're here for Mulewo," said the doorman. It was not a question. "Go to the elevator on the left."

Meromo did as he was told. The elevator was paneled with an oiled wood, and smelled fresh and sweet. It operated on voice command and quickly took him to the 63rd floor. When he emerged he found himself in an elegantly-decorated corridor, with ebony wainscotting and discreetly-placed mirrors. He walked past three unmarked doors, wondering how he was supposed to know which apartment belonged to Mulewo, and finally came to one that was partially open.

"Come in, Joseph Meromo," said a hoarse voice from within.

Meromo opened the door the rest of the way, stepped into the apartment, and blinked.

Sitting on a torn rug was an old man, wearing nothing but a red cloth gathered at the shoulder. The walls were covered by reed matting, and a noxious-smelling caldron bubbled in the fireplace. A torch provided the only illumination.

"What *is* this?" asked Meromo, ready to step back into the corridor if the old man appeared as irrational as his surroundings.

"Come sit across from me, Joseph Meromo," said the old man. "Surely this is less frightening than your nightmares."

"What do you know about my nightmares?" demanded Meromo.

"I know why you have them. I know what lies buried at the bottom of Olduvai Gorge."

Meromo shut the door quickly.

"Who told you?"

"No one told me. I have peered into your dreams, and sifted through them until I found the truth. Come sit."

Meromo walked to where the old man indicated and sat down carefully, trying not to get too much dirt on his freshly-pressed outfit.

"Are you Mulewo?" he asked.

The old man nodded. "I am Mulewo."

"How do you know these things about me?"

"I am a *laibon*," said Mulewo.

"A witch doctor?"

"It is a dying art," answered Mulewo. "I am the last practitioner."

"I thought *laibons* cast spells and created curses."

"They also remove curses—and your nights, and even your days, are cursed, are they not?"

"You seem to know all about it."

"I know that you have done a wicked thing, and that you are haunted not only by the ghost of it, but by the ghosts of the future as well."

"And you can end the dreams?"

"That is why I have summoned you here."

"But if I did such a terrible thing, why do you *want* to help me?"

"I do not make moral judgments. I am here only to help the Maasai."

"And what about the Maasai who live by the gorge?" asked Meromo. "The ones who haunt my dreams?"

"When *they* ask for help, then I will help them."

"Can you cause the material that's buried there to vanish?"

Mulewo shook his head. "I cannot undo what has been done. I cannot even assuage your guilt, for it is a just guilt. All I can do is banish it from your dreams."

"I'll settle for that," said Meromo.

There was an uneasy silence.

"What do I do now?" asked Meromo.

"Bring me a tribute befitting the magnitude of the service I shall perform."

"I can write you a check right now, or have money transferred from my account to your own."

"I have more money than I need. I must have a tribute."

"But—"

"Bring it back tomorrow night," said Mulewo.

Meromo stared at the old *laibon* for a long minute, then got up and left without another word.

He called in sick the next morning, then went to two of Dodoma's better antique shops. Finally he found what he was looking for, charged it to his personal account, and took it home with him. He was afraid to nap before dinner, so he simply read a book all afternoon, then ate a hasty meal and returned to Mulewo's apartment.

"What have you brought me?" asked Mulewo.

Meromo laid the package down in front of the old man. "A headdress made from the skin of a lion," he answered. "They told me it was worn by Sendayo himself, the greatest of all *laibons*."

"It was not," said Mulewo, without unwrapping the package. "But it is a sufficient tribute nonetheless." He reached beneath his red cloth and withdrew a small necklace, holding it out for Meromo.

"What is this for?" asked Meromo, examining the necklace. It was made of small bones that had been strung together.

"You must wear it tonight when you go to sleep," explained the old man. "It will take all your visions unto itself. Then, tomorrow, you must go to Olduvai Gorge and throw it down to the bottom, so that the visions may lay side by side with the reality."

"And that's all?"

"That is all."

Meromo went back to his apartment, donned the necklace, and went to sleep. That night his dreams were worse than they had ever been before.

In the morning he put the necklace into a pocket and had a government plane fly him to Arusha. From there he rented a ground vehicle, and two hours later he was standing on the edge of the gorge. There was no sign of the buried material.

He took the necklace in his hand and hurled it far out over the lip of the gorge.

His nightmares vanished that night.

134 years later, mighty Kilimanjaro shuddered as the long-dormant volcano within it came briefly to life.

One hundred miles away, the ground shifted on the floor of Olduvai Gorge, and three of the lead-lined containers broke open.

Joseph Meromo was long dead by that time; and, unfortunately, there were no *laibons* remaining to aid those people who were now compelled to live Meromo's nightmares.

★★★

I had examined the necklace in my own quarters, and when I came out to report my findings, I discovered that the entire camp was in a tumultuous state.

"What has happened?" I asked Bellidore.

"The Exobiologist has not returned from the gorge," he said.

"How long has she been gone?"

"She left at sunset last night. It is now morning, and she has not returned or attempted to use her communicator."

"We fear...

"...that she might..."

"...have fallen and..."

"...become immobile. Or perhaps even..."

"...unconscious..." said the Stardust Twins.

"I have sent the Historian and the Appraiser to look for her," said Bellidore.

"I can help, too," I offered.

"No, you have the last artifact to examine," he said. "When the Moriteu awakens, I will send it as well."

"What about the Mystic?" I asked.

Bellidore looked at the Mystic and sighed. "She has not said a word since landing on this world. In truth, I do not understand her function. At any rate, I do not know how to communicate with her."

The Stardust Twins kicked at the earth together, sending up a pair of reddish dust clouds.

"It seems ridiculous..." said one.

"...that we can find the tiniest artifact..." said the other.

"...but we cannot find...

"...an entire exbiologist."

"Why do you not help search for it?" I asked.

"They get vertigo," explained Bellidore.

"We searched..."

"...the entire camp," they added defensively.

"I can put off assimilating the last piece until tomorrow, and help with the search," I volunteered.

"No," replied Bellidore. "I have sent for the ship. We will leave tomorrow, and I want all of our major finds examined by then. It is *my* job to find the Exobiologist; it is *yours* to read the history of the last artifact."

"If that is your desire," I said. "Where is it?"

He led me to a table where the Historian and the Appraiser had been examining it.

"Even *I* know what this is," said Bellidore. "An unspent cartridge." He paused. "Along with the fact that we have found no human artifacts on any higher strata, I would say this in itself is unique: a bullet that a man chose *not* to fire."

"When you state it in those terms, it *does* arouse the curiosity," I acknowledged.

"Are you...

"...going to examine it...

"...now?" asked the Stardust Twins apprehensively.

"Yes, I am," I said.

"Wait!" they shouted in unison.

I paused above the cartridge while they began backing away.

"We mean..."

"...no disrespect..."

"...but watching you examine artifacts..."

"...is too unsettling."

And with that, they raced off to hide behind some of the camp structures.

"What about you?" I asked Bellidore. "Would you like me to wait until you leave?"

"Not at all," he replied. "I find diversity fascinating. With your permission, I would like to stay and observe."

"As you wish," I said, allowing my body to melt around the cartridge until it had become a part of myself, and its history became my own history, as clear and precise as if it had all occurred yesterday...

★ ★ ★

"They are coming!"

Thomas Naikosiai looked across the table at his wife.

"Was there ever any doubt that they would?"

"This was foolish, Thomas!" she snapped. "They will force us to leave, and because we made no preparations, we will have to leave all our possessions behind."

"Nobody is leaving," said Naikosiai.

He stood up and walked to the closet. "You stay here," he said, donning his long coat and his mask. "I will meet them outside."

"That is both rude and cruel, to make them stand out there when they have come all this way."

"They were not invited," said Naikosiai. He reached deep into the closet and grabbed the rifle that leaned up against the back wall, then closed the closet, walked through the airlock and emerged on the front porch.

Six men, all wearing protective clothing and masks to filter the air, confronted him.

"It is time, Thomas," said the tallest of them.

"Time for *you*, perhaps," said Naikosiai, holding the rifle casually across his chest.

"Time for all of us," answered the tall man.

"I am not going anywhere. This is my home. I will not leave it."

"It is a pustule of decay and contamination, as is this whole country," came the answer. "We are all leaving."

Naikosiai shook his head. "My father was born on this land, and his father, and his father's father. *You* may run from danger, if you wish; I will stay and fight it."

"How can you make a stand against radiation?" demanded the tall man. "Can you put a bullet through it? How can you fight air that is no longer safe to breathe?"

"Go away," said Naikosiai, who had no answer to that, other than the conviction that he would never leave his home. "I do not demand that you stay. Do not demand that I leave."

"It is for your own good, Naikosiai," urged another. "If you care nothing for your own life, think of your wife's. How much longer can she breathe the air?"

"Long enough."

"Why not let *her* decide?"

"*I* speak for our family."

An older man stepped forward. "She is *my* daughter, Thomas," he said severely. "I will not allow you to condemn her to the life you have chosen for yourself. Nor will I let my grandchildren remain here."

The old man took another step toward the porch, and suddenly the rifle was pointing at him.

"That's far enough," said Naikosiai.

"They are Maasai," said the old man stubbornly. "They must come with the other Maasai to our new world."

"You are not Maasai," said Naikosiai contemptuously. "Maasai did not leave their ancestral lands when the rinderpest destroyed their herds, or when the white man came, or when the governments sold off their lands. Maasai never surrender. *I* am the last Maasai."

"Be reasonable, Thomas. How can you not surrender to a world that is no longer safe for people to live on? Come with us to New Kilimanjaro."

"The Maasai do not run from danger," said Naikosiai.

"I tell you, Thomas Naikosiai," said the old man, "that I cannot allow you to condemn my daughter and my grandchildren to live in this hellhole. The last ship leaves tomorrow morning. They will be on it."

"They will stay with me, to build a new Maasai nation."

The six men whispered among themselves, and then their leader looked up at Naikosiai.

"You are making a terrible mistake, Thomas," he said. "If you change your mind, there is room for you on the ship."

They all turned to go, but the old man stopped and turned to Naikosiai.

"I will be back for my daughter," he said.

Naikosiai gestured with his rifle. "I will be waiting for you."

The old man turned and walked off with the others, and Naikosiai went back into his house through the airlock. The tile floor smelled of disinfectant, and the sight of the television set offended his eyes, as always. His wife was waiting for him in the kitchen, amid the dozens of gadgets she had purchased over the years.

"How can you speak with such disrespect to the Elders?" she demanded. "You have disgraced us."

"No!" he snapped. "*They* have disgraced us, by leaving!"

"Thomas, you cannot grow anything in the fields. The animals have all died. You cannot even breathe the air without a filtering mask. *Why* do you insist on staying?"

"This is our ancestral land. We will not leave it."

"But all the others—"

"They can do as they please," he interrupted. "Enkai will judge them, as He judges us all. I am not afraid to meet my creator."

"But why must you meet him so soon?" she persisted. "You have seen the tapes and disks of New Kilimanjaro. It is a beautiful world, green and gold and filled with rivers and lakes."

"Once Earth was green and gold and filled rivers and lakes," said Naikosiai. "They ruined this world. They will ruin the next one."

"Even if they do, we will be long dead," she said. "I want to go."

"We've been through all this before."

"And it always ends with an order rather than an agreement," she said. Her expression softened. "Thomas, just once before I die, I want to see water that you can drink without adding chemicals to it. I want to see antelope grazing on long green grasses. I want to walk outside without having to protect myself from the very air I breathe."

"It's settled."

She shook her head. "I love you, Thomas, but I cannot stay here, and I cannot let our children stay here."

"No one is taking my children from me!" he yelled.

"Just because you care nothing for *your* future, I cannot permit you to deny our sons *their* future."

"Their future is here, where the Maasai have always lived."

"Please come with us, Papa," said a small voice behind him, and Naikosiai turned to see his two sons, eight and five, standing in the doorway to their bedroom, staring at him.

"What have you been saying to them?" demanded Naikosiai suspiciously.

"The truth," said his wife.

He turned to the two boys. "Come here," he said, and they trudged across the room to him.

"What are you?" he asked.

"Boys," said the younger child.

"What *else*?"

"Maasai," said the older.

"That is right," said Naikosiai. "You come from a race of giants. There was a time when, if you climbed to the very top of Kilimanjaro, all the land you could see in every direction belonged to us."

"But that was long ago," said the older boy.

"Someday it will be ours again," said Naikosiai. "You must remember who you are, my son. You are the descendant of Leeyo, who killed 100 lions with just his spear; of Nelion, who waged war against the whites and drove them from the Rift; of Sendayo, the greatest of all the *laibons.* Once the Kikuyu and the Wakamba and the Lumbwa trembled in fear at the very mention of the Maasai. This is your heritage; do not turn your back on it."

"But the Kikuyu and the other tribes have all left."

"What difference does that make to the Maasai? We did not make a stand only against the Kikuyu and the Wakamba, but against *all* men who would have us change our ways. Even after the Europeans conquered Kenya and Tanganyika, they never conquered the Maasai. When Independence came, and all the other tribes moved to cities and wore suits and aped the Europeans, we remained as we had always been. We wore what we chose and we lived where we chose, for we were proud to be Maasai. Does that not *mean* something to you?"

"Will we not still be Maasai if we go to the new world?" asked the older boy.

"No," said Naikosiai firmly. "There is a bond between the Maasai and the land. We define it, and it defines us. It is what we have always fought for and always defended."

"But it is diseased now," said the boy.

"If I were sick, would you leave me?" asked Naikosiai.

"No, Papa."

"And just as you would not leave me in my illness, so we will not leave the land in *its* illness. When you love something, when it is a part of what you are, you do not leave it simply because it becomes sick. You stay, and you fight even harder to cure it than you fought to win it."

"But—

"Trust me," said Naikosiai. "Have I ever misled you?"

"No, Papa."

"I am not misleading you now. We are En-kai's chosen people. We live on the ground He has given us. Don't you see that we *must* remain here, that we must keep our covenent with En-kai?"

"But I will never see my friends again!" wailed his younger son.

"You will make new friends."

"Where?" cried the boy. "Everyone is gone!"

"Stop that at once!" said Naikosiai harshly. "Maasai do not cry."

The boy continued sobbing, and Naikosiai looked up at his wife.

"This is *your* doing," he said. "You have spoiled him."

She stared unblinking into his eyes. "Five-year-old boys are allowed to cry."

"Not Maasai boys," he answered.

"Then he is no longer Maasai, and you can have no objection to his coming with me."

"I want to go too!" said the 8-year-old, and suddenly he, too, forced some tears down his face.

Thomas Naikosiai looked at his wife and his children— really *looked* at them—and realized that he did not know them at all. This was not the quiet maiden, raised in the traditions of his people, that he had married nine years ago. These soft sobbing boys were not the successors of Leeyo and Nelion.

He walked to the door and opened it.

"Go to the new world with the rest of the black Europeans," he growled.

"Will you come with us?" asked his oldest son.

Naikosiai turned to his wife. "I divorce you," he said coldly. "All that was between us is no more."

He walked over to his two sons. "I disown you. I am no longer your father, you are no longer my sons. Now go!"

His wife puts coats and masks on both of the boys, then donned her own.

"I will send some men for my things before morning," she said.

"If any man comes onto my property, I will kill him," said Naikosiai.

She stared at him, a look of pure hatred. Then she took the children by the hands and led the out of the house and down the long road to where the ship awaited them.

Naikosiai paced the house for a few minutes, filled with nervous rage. Finally he went to the closet, donned his coat and mask, pulled out his rifle, and walked through the airlock to the front of his house. Visibility was poor, as always, and he went out to the road to see if anyone was coming.

There was no sign of any movement. He was almost disappointed. He planned to show them how a Maasai protected what was his.

And suddenly he realized that this was *not* how a Maasai protected his own. He walked to the edge of the gorge, opened the bolt, and threw his cartridges into the void one by one. Then he held the rifle over his head and hurled it after them. The coat came next, then the mask, and finally his clothes and shoes.

He went back into the house and pulled out that special trunk that held the memorabilia of a lifetime. In it he found what he was looking for: a simple piece of red cloth. He attached it at his shoulder.

Then he went into the bathroom, looking among his wife's cosmetics. It took almost half an hour to hit upon the right combinations, but when he emerged his hair was red, as if smeared with clay.

He stopped by the fireplace and pulled down the spear that hung there. Family tradition had it that the spear had once been used by Nelion himself; he wasn't sure he believed it, but it was definitely a Maasai spear, blooded many times in battle and hunts during centuries past.

Naikosiai walked out the door and positioned himself in front of his house—his *manyatta*. He planted his bare feet on the diseased ground, placed the butt of his spear next to his right foot, and stood at attention. Whatever came down the road next— an army of black Europeans hoping to rob him of his possessions, a lion out of history, a band of Nandi or Lumbwa come to slay the enemy of their blood, they would find him ready.

They returned just after sunrise the next morning, hoping convince him to emigrate to New Kilimanjaro. What they found was the last Maasai, his lungs burst from the pollution, his dead eyes staring proudly out across the vanished savannah at some enemy only he could see.

★ ★ ★

I released the cartridge, my strength nearly gone, my emotions drained.

So that was how it had ended for Man on earth, probably less than a mile from where it had begun. So bold and so foolish, so moral and so savage. I had hoped the last artifact would prove to be the final piece of the puzzle, but instead it merely added to the mystery of this most contentious and fascinating race.

Nothing was beyond their ability to achieve. One got the feeling that the moment the first primitive man looked up and saw the stars, the galaxy's days as a haven of peace and freedom were numbered. And yet they came out to the stars not just with their lusts and their hatred and their fears, but with their technology and their medicine, their heroes as well as their villains. Most of the races of the galaxy had been painted by the Creator in pastels; Men were primaries.

I had much to think about as I went off to my quarters to renew my strength. I do not know how long I lay, somnolant and unmoving, recovering my energy, but it must have been a long time, for night had come and gone before I felt prepared to rejoin the party.

As I emerged from my quarters and walked to the center of camp, I heard a yell from the direction of the gorge, and a moment later the Appraiser appeared, a large sterile bag balanced atop an air trolly.

"What have you found?" asked Bellidore, and suddenly I remembered that the Exobiologist was missing.

"I am almost afraid to guess," replied the Appraiser, laying the bag on the table.

All the members of the party gathered around as he began withdrawing items: a blood-stained communicator, bent out of shape; the floating shade, now broken, that the Exobiologist used to protect her head from the rays of the sun; a torn piece of clothing; and finally, a single gleaming white bone.

The instant the bone was placed on the table, the Mystic began screaming. We were all shocked into momentary immobility, not only because of the suddenness of her reaction, but because it was the first sign of life she had shown since joining our party. She continued to stare at the bone and scream, and finally, before we could question her or remove the bone from her sight, she collapsed.

"I don't suppose there can be much doubt about what happened," said Bellidore. "The creatures caught up with the Exobiologist somewhere on her way down the gorge and killed her."

"Probably ate..."

"...her too," said the Stardust Twins.

"I am glad we are leaving today," continued Bellidore. "Even after all these millennia, the spirit of Man continues to corrupt and degrade this world. Those lumbering creatures can't possibly be predators: there are no meat animals left on Earth. But given the opportunity, they fell upon the Exobiologist and consumed her flesh. I have this uneasy feeling that if we stayed much longer, we, too, would become corrupted by this world's barbaric heritage."

The Mystic regained consciousness and began screaming again, and the Stardust Twins gently escorted her back to her quarters, where she was given a sedative.

"I suppose we might as well make it official," said Bellidore. He turned to the Historian. "Would you please check the bone with your instruments and make sure that this is the remains of the Exobiologist?"

The Historian stared at the bone, horror-stricken. "She was my *friend*!" it said at last. "I cannot touch it as if it were just another artifact."

"We must know for sure," said Bellidore. "If it is not part of the Exobiologist, then there is a chance, however slim, that your friend might still be alive."

The Historian reached out tentatively for the bone, then jerked its hand away. "I can't!"

Finally Bellidore turned to me.

"He Who Views," he said. "Have you the strength to examine it?"

"Yes," I answered.

They all moved back to give me room, and I allowed my mass to slowly spread over the bone and engulf it. I assimilated its history and ingested its emotional residue, and finally I withdrew from it.

"It is the Exobiologist," I said.

"What are the funeral customs of her race?" asked Bellidore.

"Cremation," said the Appraiser.

"Then we shall build a fire and incinerate what remains of our friend, and we will each offer a prayer to send her soul along the Eternal Path."

And that is what we did.

The ship came later that day, and took us off the planet, and it is only now, safely removed from its influence, that I can reconstruct what I learned on that last morning.

I lied to Bellidore—to the entire party—for once I made my discovery I knew that my primary duty was to get them away from Earth as quickly as possible. Had I told them the truth, one or more of them would have wanted to remain behind, for they are scientists with curious, probing minds, and I would never be able to convince them that a curious, probing mind is no match for what I found in my seventh and final view of Olduvai Gorge.

The bone was *not* a part of the Exobiologist. The Historian, or even the Moriteu, would have known that had they not been too horrified to examine it. It was the tibia of a *man*.

Man has been extinct for five thousand years, at least as we citizens of the galaxy have come to understand him. But those lumbering, ungainly creatures of the night, who seemed so attracted to our campfires, are what Man has become. Even the pollution and radiation he spread across his own planet could not kill him off. It merely changed him to the extent that we were no longer able to recognize him.

I could have told them the simple facts, I suppose: that a tribe of these pseudo-Men stalked the Exobiologist down the gorge, then attacked and killed and, yes, ate her. Predators are not unknown throughout the worlds of the galaxy.

But as I became one with the tibia, as I felt it crashing down again and again upon our companion's head and shoulders, I felt a sense of power, of exultation I had never experienced before. I suddenly seemed to see the world through the eyes of the bone's possessor. I saw how he had killed his own companion to create the weapon, I saw how he planned to plunder the bodies of the old and the infirm for more weapons, I saw visions of conquest against other tribes living near the gorge.

And finally, at the moment of triumph, he and I looked up at the sky, and we knew that someday all that we could see would be ours.

And this is the knowledge that I have lived with for two days. I do not know who to share it with, for it is patently immoral to exterminate a race simply because of the vastness of its dreams or the ruthlessness of its ambition.

But this is a race that refuses to die, and somehow I must warn the rest of us, who have lived in harmony for almost five millennia.

*It's not over.*

## Introduction to "The Gefilte Fish Girl"

It used to be quite normal for a magazine editor to take a piece of artwork he's bought and tell one of his regular stable of writers to create a story around it.

It was a practice that had gone dormant for decades when Kristine Kathryn Rusch decided to revive it with a twist: she assigned the same piece of cover art (a cartoonish deep sea diver and a red-headed mermaid) to three of her regulars—me, Esther Friesner, and Nina Kiriki Hoffman. The three of us got together at a Nebula banquet a short time later and decided that Nina would do a horror story, Esther would do a fantasy, and I would do a science fiction.

So how do you do a science fiction story about a mermaid?

Beats me—but at least I can tell everyone I wrote the cover story.

# THE GEFILTE FISH GIRL

So I walk up to her and say, "Ma, we gotta talk."

And she never looks up from the TV, and she says, "Not during *Homemakers' Jamboree*, Marvin."

And I say, "Ma, I'm Milton. Marvin is your goniff brother who is serving 6 to 10 for passing bogus bills." (Which he is. He's a great artist, even the judge admitted that, but he just doesn't do his homework, and printing a bunch of twenties with Andrew Johnson's picture on them is probably not the brightest move he ever made.)

Anyway, she says "Marvin, Milton, what's the difference, and did you know that Liz Taylor is getting married again? What is it for her now—the 34th time?"

And I say, "You know, Ma, it's funny you should bring that up."

And she says, "Funny? Okay, Mister Big Shot, tell me what's so funny. Are you the one she's marrying? Go ahead, make my day."

And I say, "Lots of people get married, Ma. Some of them even get married to women who aren't Liz Taylor, hard as that may be for you to believe."

And she says, "Lots of *mature* people, Melvin."

And I say, "Melvin is my cousin who ran off with the gay lion tamer from the circus. I'm Milton, and speaking of mature, I'm 34 years old."

And she says, "You'd think someone who's 34 years old would know to change his socks without being told." Suddenly she curses and says, "See? You made me miss today's health tip. Here I sit, waiting to go to the hospital for a nerve transplant from all the *tsouris* you cause me, and I can't even watch my television in peace."

So I say, "You're in great shape, Ma. Every artery's as hard as a rock."

*"Feh!"* she says. "God has reserved a special place in hell for ungrateful sons."

"I know," I say. "It's probably right next to where He puts all the henpecked husbands."

"Don't you go making fun of my dear departed Erwin," she says.

"I wasn't," I say. "And besides, all we know is that he departed in one hell of a hurry. We don't know for sure that he's dead."

"If he isn't, he should be, that *momser*!" she says.

Well, I can see the thought that he may be alive and God forbid enjoying himself is about to drive her wild, so I try to mollify her.

"Okay, okay," I say, hoping the Lord is otherwise occupied and does not hear what I am about to say. "May God Himself strike me dead if he's not your late husband."

"Well, he was late for most things," she agrees, leaning back in her chair. "Except in the bedroom. Then he was early."

I try to change the subject again.

"We were talking about marriage," I say.

"Someday, when you're old enough," she says, "you'll get married and ruin some poor Jewish girl's happiness, just the way your dear departed father ruined mine, and the only good thing that will come of it will be a grandson who, knock wood, won't take after his father and his grandfather but will show me a little respect and compassion."

I begin to see that this is going to be even more difficult than I thought, and I try to come up with a subtle way to break the news to her. So I think, and I think, and I think some more, and finally I say, as subtly as I can, "Ma, I'm engaged."

And she looks away from the television set and takes her feet off the hassock and plants them on the floor, and stares at me for maybe 30 seconds, and finally she says, "Engaged to do what?"

"To get married," I say.

She digs into her sewing kit, which is on the floor next to her, and pulls out a scissors.

"Here," she says, handing it to me. "Why waste all afternoon rushing me to the hospital's cardiac unit? Just stab me now and be done with it."

"Jugular or varicose?" I ask.

*"Schmendrick!"* she says. "How can the fruit of my looms talk to me like this?"

"I'm the fruit of your loins, Ma," I tell her. "Fruit of the Loom is what I'm wearing beneath my pants."

"All right," she says. "Just stand there and watch me breathe my last."

"Your last what?" I ask.

She glares at me and finally says, "Before I die, at least tell me the name of this female person you're engaged to do whatever with."

"Melora of the Purple Mist," I say.

"Melora of the Purple Mist?" she repeats. "How can I fit all that on a wedding invitation?"

"Just use Melora," I say.

"And what bowling alley or topless club do you meet Miss Whats-her-name of the Purple Mist at?" she asks.

"I met her at work, kind of," I answer.

"I *knew* it!" she says, poking a pudgy forefinger into the air. "I knew I should never let you take that job with the sewage company!"

"It's a salvage company," I say.

"Sewage, salvage, what's the difference?" she demands. "It's that Gypsy who walks around half-naked with her deathless beauty sagging down to her *pupik*, right? I *told* you she had her sights set on you!"

"She's not a Gypsy, and it's not her. She's just another diver."

"So you're marrying some other girl who lies around on deck with her *tuchus* soaking up the sun," she says. "I should feel better about that?"

"She doesn't lie around on deck," I say uneasily.

"On deck, below deck, big difference," she snaps.

"Bigger than you think," I say. "The truth of it is, she spends most of her time about 50 feet below deck."

"So she's a diver," she says.

"Not exactly," I answer.

"What, then?"

"Try not to get real excited, Ma," I say.

"I'm not excited, I have convulsions all the time," she says. "Just tell me."

"She's a mermaid," I say.

"As long as she's not that Gypsy girl," she says, fanning herself with the *TV Guide*. "Or that lady bartender from last summer. Or the bug woman."

"The entomologist," I correct her.

"Whatever," she says. "So tell me about this Purple Mist person."

"Like I said, she's a mermaid."

"Like what has a tail and spends her whole life in the water?" she asks.

"That's right," I say.

"Does she wear a bra?" she says suddenly.

"Ma!" I say, outraged.

"You heard me—does she wear a bra?"

"No," I finally answer.

"Figures," she says.

"What a thing to ask!" I say.

"What do you want me to ask?" she says. "My son comes home and tells me he's marrying someone who's covered with scales and spends all her time swimming in salt water, despite what it must do to her complexion. So can she at least get us a price on fresh fish?"

"It's not something I'm real concerned with," I say.

"Of course not," she says. "You're as impractical as your dear, departed father." She sighs. "All right, so where did this female person go to school?"

"I don't think she did," I say.

"Ah!" she says with an knowing nod. "Rich family with a private tutor. What temple do they belong to?"

"Who?"

"Her family," she says. "Try to pay attention, Martin."

"Martin is your nephew who went broke manufacturing the folding waterbed," I say. "I'm Milton, remember?"

"Don't change the subject," she says. "What temple do they go to?"

"They don't," I say.

"They're Reformed?" she asks.

I take a deep breath and say, "They're not Jewish at all," and then I wait for the explosion.

It takes about three one-millionths of a second—a new record.

"You're marrying a *shiksa*?" she bellows.

"I'm marrying a mermaid," I say.

"Who cares about *that*?" she screams. "Call my doctor! I'm having a coronary!"

"Ma, try to understand—there *aren't* any Jewish mermaids," I say.

"It's *my* fault?" she demands. "It's bad enough that you want to give me grandsons with fins—and how in the world will the rabbi perform the *bris*?—but now you tell me that their mother's a *goy*?"

"I knew I was gonna have trouble with you," I say unhappily.

"Trouble?" she shrieks. "Why should there be trouble? Your Uncle Nate will come by with a knife and a cracker and say, 'Is this a jar of Baluga caviar?', and I'll say 'No, it's 40,000 of my grandchildren.'"

"Will you at least meet her?" I ask.

"Some conversation we'll have," she replied. "She'll say 'Blub!' I'll say 'Gurgle!' and she'll say 'Glub!' and I'll say 'I'm getting the folds', and she'll say—"

"That's the bends, not the folds," I explain.

"Bends, folds, what's the difference?" she says. "I plan to be dead of a heart attack in two more minutes."

"She speaks English," I say, getting back to the subject.

"She does?"

"With a beautiful lilting accent."

"I knew it!" she says. "You're too young to remember, but they drove our people out of Lilting before the last war..."

"Lilting isn't a place, Ma," I say.

"It isn't?" she says suspiciously. "Are you sure of that?"

"I'm sure," I say. "She really wants to meet you."

"I'll just bet she does," she says. "She probably wants to feed me to her pet lobster."

"I don't think lobsters eat people," I say.

"Aha!" she says. "But you don't *know*!"

"We're getting off the subject," I say.

"Right," she agrees. "The subject was my imminent death."

"The subject was Melora."

"What does this fish person who doesn't wear a bra want with you anyway?" she demands. "Why doesn't she go elope with some nice halibut?"

"I met her while I was hunting for treasure," I say. "It was love at first sight."

"So what you're saying is that you went down there looking for gold and what you came up with was a female person of the Purple Mist?"

"You're making this very difficult, Ma."

"You bring home a cod for dinner, and instead of cooking it I have to give it my son, and *I'm* making this difficult?" she says, just a bit hysterically.

I figure it's time to play my ace in the hole, so I say, "She's willing to convert, Ma."

"Into what—a woman with two or more legs?"

"To Judaism," I say. "I told her how important it was to you."

"How can she convert?" she says. "Do we know any rabbis who can hold services 50 feet under the water?"

"She can come to the surface," I say. "How else would we talk?"

"When did you ever *talk* to a girl?" she says. "You're just like your departed father."

"We talk all the time," I say.

She considers this and finally nods her head. "I suppose there's not a lot else you can do."

"Don't get personal, Ma," I say.

She raises her eyes to the heavens—which are just beyond the lightbulb in the middle of the ceiling—and has another of her hourly chats with God. "He wants me to welcome a lady fish into my family and he tells me not to get personal."

"A lady Jewish fish," I point out.

"So okay, she won't be just a fish girl, she'll be a gefilte fish girl, big deal. What do I feed her? If I give her lox, will she accuse me of cooking her relatives?"

"She eats fish all the time, Ma."

"And when we leave the table to go watch Oprah, do I carry her or does she slither on her belly?"

"Actually, she doesn't watch Oprah," I say.

"She doesn't watch Oprah?" she says, and I can tell this shocks her more than the fact that Melora is a mermaid. "What's wrong with her?"

"She's never seen a television," I say. "They don't have them in her kingdom."

"What are they, some kind of Communists?" she demands.

"They don't have any electricity," I explain.

"You mean she doesn't even have a food processor?"

"That's right," I say.

"That poor girl!" she says. "And no disposal unit in her sink?"

"None," I say, and I can see that suddenly she's working up a head of sympathy.

"How can anybody live like that?" she says.

"She manages just fine."

"Nonsense!" she says. "Nobody can live without a trash masher. My son's wife may be a fish, but she isn't going to slave 30 hours a day just because *I* had to!"

"That's very thoughtful, Ma," I say. "But—"

"Don't interrupt!" she snaps. "You bring her by this afternoon. I'll have some knishes ready, and some blintzes, and maybe a little chopped liver, and we'll watch Oprah and I'll show her my kitchen and..." Suddenly she stops and re-thinks her schedule. "Bring her earlier and we can watch Donahue, too. And tonight they're re-running that old series with Lloyd Bridges. It should make her feel right at home."

"You'll like her, Ma," I promise.

"Like, *shmike*," she says. "If I have to go through life without ever being able to point to my son the doctor, at least I can point to my almost-daughter the gefilte fish girl. Mrs. Noodleman down the block will be so jealous!" She pauses. "We'll have to put a little meat on her bones."

"You haven't even seen her," I say.

"That's all right," she says. "I know your taste in women. Cheap and skinny."

"Ma, you think any woman under 200 pounds is skinny."

"And you think any woman who doesn't ask for ice cubes and a straw with her wine is sophisticated." She gets up, and I can see she's getting set for a couple of hours of serious puttering. "Now, you go get her and bring her back, while I prepare something for the poor undernourished thing to eat. And I think I'll invite Rabbi Bernstein, since we need someone to work with her, and he's always fishing when he should be at Temple, and..."

As I leave, she is trying to remember which company sells the pens that write under water so she can send out wedding invitations to the bride's family.

## Introduction to "Lady in Waiting"

Originally I was just going to edit *Alternate Kennedys*, not write for it as well. But as the stories began coming in, and I realized the book had at least three or four pieces that were lead-pipe cinches to make either the Hugo or the Nebula ballot, I decided I wanted to be a contributor as well as an editor.

Most of the stories were about Joe and his sons and daughters. I decided to write about a waitress named Norma Jean who never became Marilyn Monroe, but attracted the attentions of the President anyway.

# LADY IN WAITING

Her name is Norma Jean Baker, and she has been sitting by her telephone for four days and three nights.

It seems like only an hour ago that she was in the West Wing of the White House, her arms and legs wrapped around the President as he attacked his goal with his characteristic vigor. Then it was a glass of wine, a few shared words, and she was ushered out, down the elevator, through the basement, down a corridor, up another elevator, and out the door of the Executive Office Building to the waiting limosine.

*You are the greatest,* the President had said. *Baby, I've been around and you are the best. I've got to see you again.*

*But you're a married man, Mr. President,* she had replied.

*Not for long,* he said. *As soon as the election's over, she's history.* He smiled his charismatic smile. *Don't make any long-term plans, okay?*

*When will I see you again?* she asked.

*Soon,* he replied, lighting a cigar and starting to put his clothes on. *I'll call you tomorrow.*

She went home and spent the whole night thinking of the vistas that had opened up for her in the President's bedroom. There would be formal dinners and ball gowns, private concerts by Sinatra and the President's other Hollywood buddies, even parties by the swimming pools at the family compound in...in *wherever* it was that they all lived when they weren't in Washingon.

She'd have to watch her figure, of course. So many politician's wives let themselves go to pot once their husbands started hitting the banquet circuit. She made up her mind that she wouldn't be one of them; she'd never give him reason to be embarrassed by her. She'd even go to the library and start reading all about politics and things like that, so they'd have interesting things to talk about. She was really going to work at being the kind of woman he needed, and she planned to tell him that as soon as he called her.

But the phone didn't ring. She had stayed in the apartment, afraid to go out for food, afraid even to leave the phone long enough to visit the bathroom. But the call hadn't come, and finally she turned on the television to see what crisis had developed to keep him away from the phone.

But there was nothing on the news. Martin Luther King had given another speech, Fidel Castro had made another threat, Sandy Koufax had pitched another shutout. The President was there, of course, welcoming the head of some African country, but that only took him a few minutes.

Still, he *was* the President, and if she was going to marry him, she would have to get used to the fact that Presidents had, well, presidential things to do.

She stayed up until midnight, then set the alarm for seven o'clock and went to bed.

She got up before the alarm went off and sat by the telephone. At nine in the morning she called the phone company to make sure her number was working. At eleven she realized that she had no food in the house, and paid a neighbor to watch the phone while she ran out to the store. She was back forty minutes later, and didn't really believe the neighbor when she informed her that there had been no calls.

What was the matter?

His wife must be back from that trip. Yes, she had decided, that must be it.

But how often does his wife visit the Oval Office?

But his secretary is there, and he doesn't want *her* to know.

But he's the President. He could order her to leave.

But there's his brother. Can he order *him* to leave?

But his brother has his own office at the Justice Department.

Then it must be his back, she decided. It had been bothering him when she had arrived. Probably he was in too much pain to call. Probably he was in bed, writhing in discomfort. The poor baby.

But he was on the television again that night, and his back didn't seem to be bothering him at all. He was giving a speech in New York, and of course that was why he hadn't called her.

She frowned.

The President of the United States couldn't make a phone call from New York?

People were watching him.

From the bedroom of his private suite?

He didn't have her number.

But he had only flown up there in late afternoon, and he was home already.

She looked at herself in the mirror. Approvingly. He would call. After all, he had picked her out from all the women in Washington, and he wasn't just some horny middle-aged businessman looking for a quick roll in the hay: he was the President of the United States. He wasn't interested in an endless supply of bimbos; he had too much class for that. His marriage was in trouble, he had seen her, and something had just clicked.

*You ought to dye your hair blonde,* he had said. *Pose for some cheesecake shots, maybe go into movies.*

*Norma Jean Baker isn't a movie star's name,* she had pointed out.

*So you'll change it,* he replied. *Something catchy and alliterative.* Then he had smiled. *No one would dare say no to Norma Jean Kennedy.*

She waited by the phone until two in the morning, then fell asleep without setting the alarm. She slept until noon, then practically jumped out of her chair when the phone rang.

"I've been waiting for your call," she said in her breathiest voice.

But it had been a bored woman wanting to know if she needed her chimney cleaned at bargain rates, and she had slammed the phone down so hard that she thought for a moment she might have broken it, so she called the phone company again and insisted that they call her back, which they did half an hour later, startling her again as she was cooking some eggs.

At four o'clock she walked to her closet and began going through her wardrobe. The tight sweaters and tighter skirts were nice, very eye-catching, no question about it, but as the wife of a President she'd need something a little better, a little classier. Maybe she should start going through the Sears and Ward's catalogs. Some shirtwaists, perhaps, and a lowcut evening gown or two. After all, she would be making trips abroad as *his* representative, and she'd have to look her best.

She looked at her hair in the mirror. Maybe it *was* time to go blonde. And to pick up a book or two on how to speak French and Spanish.

At six o'clock she called Weather, to make sure the phone was still fuctioning, then broke the connection for fear a call might be coming in from the White House at that very instant.

She turned on Walter Cronkite at 6:30. Usually the news bored her, but now things were different: she was going to have to learn who her husband's friends and enemies were, what countries we were courting and which ones we were threatening. And then there was the family. She would start by charming the Attorney General—he looked like the hardest case—and then, once she'd won him over, she'd meet all the sisters. She didn't know quite what she'd talk about with them, but one of them had married an actor, so they had *something* in common. She could discuss the current heartthrobs with the best of them.

At ten o'clock in the evening she called the White House.

"May I help you?" asked the operator.

*What do I tell her?*

She hung up without saying a word.

At 10:45 she called again.

"May I help you?"

"I'd like to speak to the President, please."

"The President isn't available. Where may I direct your call?"

"I've got to speak to *him* personally."

"What is the nature of your business?"

*I want to know why he hasn't called me?*

"It's personal."

"If you'll please leave your name and number..."

She hung up again.

*He must have a private number.* She could find it. There was that guy from the phone company who kept looking down her dress, what was his name, Paul? Yes, Paul. She could call Paul and get it from him.

*Did people call the President? Did he have a private line in his bedroom, or only the hotline with Russia? And what if his wife picked it up?*

She was still pondering her options when she fell asleep.

This morning she wakes up with the sun. For the first time since she left the White House she thinks about her job. Probably she'd already been fired. No great loss; she will never work as a waitress again.

She wonders idly what kind of job the President's current wife had when they met, whether she'll go back to work after he leaves her, whether later on they can become friends. There are so many things she has to learn about him, and about being a First Lady. It would be nice to have someone to ask, someone who's been through it all.

She realizes that she is chewing gum, and self-consciously takes it out of her mouth. That habit will have to go, she decides regretfully; you simply don't chew gum at all the state dinners and fancy parties a President's wife must attend.

She thinks back on her three hours in the West Wing, as she has done a hundred times since returning to her apartment. This is a classy man, this President. He carries himself so well, he dresses so elegantly, he knows all the right wines, the right things to say. His manners are impeccable, much more of a Clark Gable than a Humphrey Bogart or a John Wayne. He doesn't smoke in public, but he has a supply of very expensive Havanas in his room. Nothing second-rate about him.

Of course, he wasn't that great in bed, in truth he seemed more concerned with his own pleasure than hers, but he is the President, he carries the hopes and fears of the Free World on his broad shoulders, and she's sure that things will improve once they start sleeping together on a regular basis. He will learn to relax, to not be in such a hurry; she will see to it.

Their relationship will have to be kept secret for a while longer, she knows. He can't afford a scandal before he is re-elected, and she will have to live with the situation. It won't be her first secret relationship; a lot of Washington businessmen and lawyers that she's known have had wives. Most of them, in fact.

But they never promised to marry her, and *he* did. At least, she *thinks* he did. *Don't make any long-term plans,* he had said. What else could that have meant? His wife will be history after the election. Those were his very words: she's history. Why shouldn't she believe him? What reason could he have to lie to her?

But he had also promised to call, and it's been more than three days.

*He's the most important man in the world,* she tells herself. *He'll call. He's surrounded by advisors and generals and things. He just has to get a moment alone.*

And if he's had second thoughts? If he doesn't want to marry her, just set her up as his mistress?

She considers the matter coldly. He's still the President. If that's what he wants, she can adjust to it. He's worth millions; a brownstone in Georgetown wouldn't be so hard to take. Diamonds now and then. A couple of charge cards at the better stores. Fine meals, fine wines, classy new friends who talk about politics and philosophy and opera and things like that.

Yes, she can live with it. All he has to do is call.

She stares at her phone.

It doesn't ring.

*What is keeping you?* she wants to know. *Don't you know I've been waiting for almost four days?*

She studies her face and figure in the mirror again, and now she reassures her unhappy image: *Smile, Norma Jean. You're not just some unimportant waitress any more. The President of the United States thought enough of you to bring you to the White House itself. Can any other woman can make that claim?*

She reads a movie magazine, watches a quiz show, drinks a pair of beers. The sun begins going down. She realizes that she's very tense, very edgy. She ought to pop down to the drug store and pick up some sleeping pills, but then she would have to leave the apartment.

She considers putting on her coat and going out, then shakes her head and sits down again by the phone.

"It'll ring," she says. "Any minute now, it'll ring. He'll tell me why he couldn't get away sooner, and then we'll make an arrangement to meet again."

At midnight she cannot keep her eyes open any longer.

"Tomorrow," she murmers just before she falls into a restless sleep. "He'll call tomorrow."

## Introduction to "Stanley the Eighteen-Percenter"

I was editing an anthology called *Deals With the Devil* for DAW Books, and I decided to write a story for it myself, since I knew the editor was incredibly partial to Resnick stories.

I figured everyone else would do classic biter-bit stories (as we in the biz refer to them), so I thought I'd take a different approach.

# STANLEY, THE EIGHTEEN-PERCENTER

Lots of people get ten or fifteen percent: literary agents, theatrical agents, business managers, and various other assorted flesh peddlers. Some of them are worth it, most of them aren't...but ten to fifteen percent is the going rate.

So it should go without saying that Stanley Mitterwald is a little out of the ordinary. He is an eighteen-percenter—the *only* eighteen-percenter—and he's worth every penny of it.

You don't read about him much, because he likes to keep out of the limelight, but you certainly know his clients. He's the guy who got Ibn Jad el Khobar six million dollars to jump from India to Pakistan in the Pan-Asian Soccer League. And remember when Billy McBrine signed a twenty-year no-cut pact with the Yankees after every specialist in the country said his arm wouldn't last out the year? Stanley's doing. And of course, he's the guy who invented the Hollywood play-or-pay deal.

Yeah, he's one hell of a sharp guy. Made his first ten million in sports before he branched out, but he soon got into just about everything.

So he was probably a little less surprised than he should have been when the statuesque redhead walked into his office and plumped herself down in the chair across from his desk.

"May I help you?" asked Stanley in his most ingratiating yet businesslike tone of voice.

"I certainly hope so," was the reply. "I'm really quite desperate, Mr. Mitterwald, and I've been told that you are the one man I can turn to."

"Are you in the performing arts, Miss...I'm afraid I didn't catch your name?"

"Not precisely," she said. "And my name is Lilith."

"Ah, a BIblical name," he said with a smile. "And a rare one at that."

"Also Jezebel," she continued. "And Bathsheba, and Desiree, and Mata Hari, and Big-Nosed Kate, and Christine Keeler, and..." The list went on and on, but Stanley prided himself on his professional etiquette and managed to hear her out with nothing more than an occasional sage and sympathetic nod of his balding head.

"And what can I do for you, Ms. Lilith?" he asked when the litany had finally ended.

"My working conditions are intolerable."

"I see," said Stanley, pursing his lips thoughtfully and juxtaposing his fingers. "Just what line of work are you in?"

"My duties are rather loosely defined," replied Lilith. "Perhaps if I showed you my contract...?"

"That might be best," agreed Stanley, repressing an urge to paw his carpet and bay the moon.

She reached into her purse, withdrew an ancient rolled parchment, and handed it over to him. Stanley almost did a double-take when he came to the signatures—one in blood and the other burned on with a cloven hoof—but he controlled himself most admirably. He forced himself to read the brief contract twice before looking up with an expression of fury on his sallow face.

"This is outrageous!" he said. "No hospitalization, no sick days, no personal days, no vacation time—and your salary has been frozen for nine hundred and forty-one centuries!" He gulped down a deep breath. "Absolutely outrageous!"

"Do you think that you will be able to help me?" she asked hopefully.

"I certainly intend to try," said Stanley firmly. "It's not exactly my field of expertise, but an unfair contract is an unfair contract no matter who issues it." He paused. "Now tell me, Ms. Lilith—do you want out altogether?"

"Oh, no!" she said quickly, with a sudden passion in her voice. "I love my work."

"I see," said Stanley, lowering his head in thought and wondering why his throat had suddenly become so dry.

"It's just my contract that I want to change," Lilith continued. "I mean, there's a difference between being a working girl and a piece of chattel, don't you agree?"

"Indeed," said Stanley, noticing that his palms were beginning to sweat. "Indeed there is."

"I wish I could think of *some* way to show my appreciation," said Lilith suggestively. "After all, it isn't everyone who would accept a client in my particular line of endeavor."

"My dear young lady," said Stanley, "morals, lifestyles and occupations are of little consequence to me. I deal in contracts."

And with that, he launched into such a rhapsodic dissertation on the beauty, nature and complexity of contracts that he quite forgot that he was speaking to the most beautiful and seductive woman who had ever lived. Or died.

*"Oy!"* said Lucifer, running a pudgy pink hand through his thinning gray hair. "Renegotiate? As if I didn't have *tsouris* enough." He stared at Stanley across his polished obsidian desk. "What's a nice Jewish boy like you doing in a place like this, anyway?"

"My client," said Stanley, who found himself curiously unimpressed with the devil, "has asked me to represent her in these discussions. May I suggest that you take a look at this?"

He tossed a copy of his proposal onto the desk. Lucifer picked it up, moaned while reading through it, and finally placed it back on the desk. "Stanley, what kind of *goniff* are you?" he demanded.

"I beg your pardon?" said Stanley.

"How could you strike at my heart like this?" said Lucifer plaintively. "What have I ever done to you? Do I put cockroaches in your *borsht*? Do I sneak pork into your *gefilte* fish? Do I make that hideous Mrs. Yingleman from down the block fall in love with you?" Lucifer held up a hand. "No, it's all right, God forbid you should respond in kind. I'll just sit here in the dark while you and that redheaded *yenta* plot my downfall."

Stanley simply stared at Lucifer without speaking.

"So *nu*?" demanded Lucifer. "So now what's wrong, you aren't even enough of a *mensch* to talk to me?"

"I think what it is..." began Stanley hesitantly. "That is, I was expecting a more traditional type of devil."

*"Oy,"* muttered Lucifer. "So now I have to be a traditional devil because Stanley the Big Shot insists." He grunted once, seemed to strain as if under supreme dynamic tension, and suddenly he was transformed into a huge, horned, hairy crimson being equipped with tail, hooves and a pitchfork.

"More to your liking?" asked Lucifer.

"I suppose so," said Stanley. "But somehow you still seem to lack character."

*"Momser!"* muttered Lucifer. He tensed and grunted once more, and immediately developed a facial tic, a hairlip, warts, and halitosis. "Satisfactory?"

Stanley's idea of character didn't agree with Lucifer's, but since he worked on commission rather than an hourly scale he decided not to spend any more time trying to get the devil to look like upper level management. Therefore he nodded his approval, pulled out his briefcase, and laid a number of documents on the desk.

"Now I feel, at the outset, that we should lay our cards on the table," began Stanley. "My client has a list of non-negotiable demands that must be agreed to before we can proceed any further."

Lucifer thumbed through the demands, his eyes wide and staring. "Cost of living increase...retroactive vacation pay...major medical... *air-conditioning*? This list is unacceptable!"

"You must understand, sir," said Stanley patiently, "that these are not requests, but demands. They must all be conceded before we can even begin to discuss the various other clauses and riders."

"And if I say no?" said Lucifer ominously.

"Before I arrived here, I took a little excursion through your outer office," said Stanley calmly.

"So?"

"And I pointed out some of the advantages to be gained by collective bargaining," he said. "I now represent not only Lilith, but CD&D as well."

"CD&D?" repeated Lucifer.

"The Brotherhood of Consolidated Devils and Demons, Limited."

*"Oy!"* moaned Lucifer. "As if I didn't have *tsouris* enough!"

Stanley had a curious intimation that this would be his longest and hardest bargaining session, that it would go on for days and days, and that he was facing one hell of a tough customer. Still, he had a duty to his clients and a sense of devotion to the high ideals of his profession, so he lowered his head and plunged straight forward.

"First of all," he said, "we're going to have to decide on our agenda, once we get past the basic package. Now, I'd like to move on to medical benefits next, but if you'd prefer overtime compensation or production bonuses or..."

Lucifer's eyes began glazing over with a combination of self-pity and resignation.

★ ★ ★

Stanley was sitting in his new suite of offices, putting the final touches on Jolting Jim Jefferson's contract for his heavyweight title defense, when he suddenly became aware of a presence behind him. He turned and found himself confronting Lucifer in his pitchfork-and-brimstone persona.

Stanley swallowed hard once, then regained his composure and met the devil's eyes. "Did you have an appointment?"

Lucifer looked flustered and shook his head.

"No matter," said Stanley with a shrug. "Any grievance you may have with CD&D must go through normal channels anyway."

"That's not why I'm here," said Lucifer uneasily.

"Oh?"

"A very long time ago," continued the devil, "I did a rather silly thing."

"So I've been informed," said Stanley dryly.

"It was an act of youthful impetuosity, nothing more," said Lucifer. "A foolish juvenile folly, and I've regretted it deeply ever since."

"Yes?" replied Stanley noncommittally.

"Well," said Lucifer, shifting his hooves nervously and looking at the floor, "I've decided that the time has come to sue for peace."

"And you need a representative?" said Stanley.

Lucifer nodded. "I'm afraid I'm not allowed at their conference table."

"I see."

"I need a really tough negotiator, someone who can get me the best possible terms."

"I think you've made the right decision," said Stanley with just the proper touch of professional detachment. He informed his secretary that he was not to be disturbed, lit a cigar, and pulled out a pen and a pad of yellow paper. "Now, just what concessions are you willing to make and which areas shall we consider to be non-negotiable?"

And, moment later, Stanley was happily immersed in the writing of his latest contract.

## Introduction to "Slice of Life"

Back when Tappan King was editing *Twilight Zone*, he asked me to contribute a horror story.

I had never written one before (and for what it's worth, I've never written one since). I just can't buy the standard tropes of horror: vampires, harpies, wolfmen, and the like.

But I did come up with one idea that seemed worth the effort, so I wrote it up and sold it to Tappan.

It appeared in the last-ever issue of *Twilight Zone*. I hope it wasn't my fault.

# SLICE OF LIFE

He called himself Ellery Curtis, but that was not his real name.

The first time he saw the golden fog, he was shaving, staring at his pale blue eyes in the bathroom mirror. The fog took shape about fifteen feet behind him, somewhere in the adjoining bedroom.

He jumped, startled, and put a deep gash in his chin. Unmindful of the pain, he threw his razor into the sink and turned to face the bedroom.

"Who's there?" he demanded.

There was no response. He walked carefully into the bedroom and began searching, looking behind the old leather recliner that had seen better days, inside his small narrow closet, under the beat-up four-poster that had come with the apartment.

He opened a dresser drawer, pulled out a .38 automatic, uncapped the safety, and made a careful tour of the apartment's four small rooms. He found nothing.

Shrugging, he returned to the bathroom and applied a styptic pencil to his chin. He washed, dressed, and walked to the kitchen to prepare breakfast...and had the unearthly feeling of being watched.

He raced across the kitchen and burst into the bedroom. He thought he saw a trace of gold out of the corner of his eye, somewhere in the vicinity of the window, but when he turned to look at it, it was gone.

He checked the window latches. Bolted.

He checked the door. Locked.

And, because yellow fogs aren't exactly the norm for housebreakers, he checked the fireplace flue. Closed.

He was sweating now, and his chin began stinging, but he forced himself to finish his breakfast. He debated tucking the pistol in his belt but decided that bullets were't all that useful against an overactive and undercontrolled imagination and left it at home.

He spent the next three hours teaching judo and karate to flabby housewives whose fears were probably as groundless as their talents and, at noon, he took a quick shower and prepared to go out for lunch—and saw it again, more clearly this time.

It hung a few inches above the floor of the locker room, oblivious to air currents, and yet not without its own internal movement, as if this enormous mass of translucence were trying to *become* something.

Curtis remained motionless for an instant, then threw a water glass at the fog. It vanished, and the glass smashed into a thousand fragments against the tiled wall. Curtis walked over to where it had been, hoping to find some trace of it. The room seemed exactly as it had before, with nothing but the broken pieces of glass to give testimony that anything out of the ordinary had occurred.

He stood motionless, waiting, but the fog did not return. Finally he shrugged and walked back to his locker, muttering a brief "Damn!" as his bare foot came down on a sharp fragment of glass. He sat down on a bench, pulled the glass out of his foot, got a bandage from the first-aid kit, and dressed.

He walked slowly through the building, past the tumbling mats and the plush desk in the reception room, but saw nothing unusual. Finally he walked out on the sidewalk. The teeming mass of humanity scurrying by him made him feel a sense of relief and security. He was back in the real world, where the only fogs were those that came off the ocean at night.

He walked the three blocks to his usual restaurant, picking up a newspaper and greeting an occasional acquaintance along the way. He was about twenty feet from the doorway when he saw it again, a little less shapeless than before.

It filled the entrance, glowing a dull gold, shimmering slightly, still seeking a form that seemed beyond its grasp. Curtis, shaking violently, looked around to see if anyone else had noticed it. A small, fiftyish woman who had been walking beside him continued on into the restaurant, walking right through the pulsating fog. Curtis shook his head and rubbed his eyes; when he looked up, it was gone.

Suddenly food was the last thing he wanted. Instead, his hands still trembling, he pulled a small address booklet out of his pocket.

"Ellery," said the lean, gray-haired woman, looking at him over the top of her horn-rimmed glasses. "I must say I hadn't expected to see you at this late date."

"Ditto," said Curtis. "But I seem to have another problem."

"Another?" said Doctor Edith Stillpass, chewing absently on the end of a pencil. "Or is it simply a different manifestation of the same one?"

He shook his head vigorously. "It's nothing like before: no headaches, no nightmares, nothing like that at all."

"Have a seat and tell me what it *is* like," said Edith, checking her appointment book and deciding that she could spare Curtis fifteen or twenty minutes without falling too far behind her schedule.

"It's kind of hard to describe," he said, ignoring the chair and pacing nervously up and down the office instead. "It's like...well, like a golden mist."

"You're having dreams about a golden mist?"

*"No!"* he yelled, and the sound of his voice seemed to startle him. "I apologize. I didn't mean to shout. But it's not a dream. I see it when I'm shaving, when I'm showering. I even saw it when I went out to lunch."

"A gold-colored mist?"

He nodded.

"What does it do7" asked Edith.

"Nothing," said Curtis.

"Nothing?"

"Yet," he said with a shudder.

"What do you think it *will* do?"

"How the hell should I know?"

"Has anyone else seen it?"

"No."

"And you've had no nightmares since our last conversation?"

"None," said Curtis. "I've been fine. Until this morning, anyway."

"By the way, Ellery," said Edith, "what happened to your chin? That's a nasty cut you've got there."

"It startled me while I was shaving."

"I see. But it didn't touch you or speak to you?"

"No. Does it make any sense to you at all?"

"Well, Ellery," she began, "if you want my honest opinion, I think you were hallucinating."

"No! I saw it!"

"Let me continue. We both know that you had a dreadful experience fifteen years ago, an experience that drove you completely off the deep end for a number of months and required almost four years of treatment."

"I don't see what that has to do with this," said Curtis.

"Ellery, you were forced to watch a brutal, senseless slaughter of innocent women and children. It made no difference that you weren't involved in the Quang Chai Massacre, that you tried to prevent your officers from precipitating this horrible bloodbath. Your mind couldn't face the reality of what it had seen, and you became semi-catatonic And even after that phase had passed, you had headaches and nightmares for years. Your subconscious kept repeating the scene, often with exceptionally gruesome and fictitious embellishments. Hallucinations are funny things, Ellery; we consider them relatively normal when they come to us in the guise of dreams, and totally abnormal when they come to us during our waking hours. But there's not all that much difference between them, truly there's not. This mist of yours leaves no trace, is seen by no one else, comes and goes when you least expect it. That certainly sounds like an hallucination to me."

"But it seemed so real!" stammered Curtis.

"That's the nature of hallucinations," smiled Edith. "If they seemed unreal, who would believe in them?" She pulled out a note pad and began scribbling on it with her pencil. "I'm going to prescribe a rather strong tranquilizer for you, Ellery. Take it just before going to sleep, and drop by again on..." She checked a calendar on her desk. "How about two in the afternoon, a week from today?"

He nodded, mumbled his thanks, took the prescription, and left.

And went home.

And took a tranquilizer and washed it down with a vodka stinger.

And tried to sleep.

The room danced with moonbeams, stray strands of light peeping in over the neighboring buildings.

Curtis awoke with a start, took a deep breath, then lay back slowly on his pillow. It had been a nightmare, his first in years. In it he saw yellow and olive bodies cut in half by a knife of bullets, heard the shrieks of the children, smelled the sicksweet odor of quarts and gallons of bright red blood, tasted the acrid smoke of gunpowder.

He knew that he must still be dreaming, for the cloud of gunpowder now hovered above him, spreading through the air like some supernatural creature of the night.

But gunpowder was smoke and gray, and this *thing* was golden.

He tried to scream and found that he couldn't. His limbs felt numb, whether from fear or the medication, and he lay helpless on his back as the golden mist approached him, still striving without success to form itself into *something*.

Its nearness chilled him to the bone. It slithered over him, substanceless yet horribly cold. Finally his body responded to his mind and he leaped from the bed. He turned to confront the mist, and was half surprised to find that it was still there. He aimed a swift kick at its middle, and felt his foot go right through it. As he regained his balance he somehow sensed a feeling of mirth emanating from the mist.

He prepared to attack again, and the golden mist began retreating toward the window. He dove at it and it vanished, leaving his hand feeling numb with cold.

He turned on all the lights in the apartment and began walking from room to room, though he knew he wouldn't find it. As he returned to his bedroom, he sensed that something was different, and commenced a methodical search, trying to pinpoint what had changed.

He was on the verge of giving up when his eyes fell upon the locked window. It was covered with a fine mist, as if his air conditioner had been left on for too long, and written, as if by a finger, on the mist, in a fine delicate hand, was a number:

998

"I'll be honest with you, Ellery," said Edith Stillpass. "I haven't the slightest idea what it means. You're sure you saw it there?"

"Absolutely."

"You don't mind if I try to analyze it as if it were a dream, do you7"

"I mind like all hell, but I suppose you're going to do it anyway."

"I am," smiled Edith. "Why 998? Does the number have any special significance to you?"

"None."

"How many people died at Quang Chai?"

"Eighty," said Curtis.

Edith frowned. "How many days did you serve in Viet Nam?"

"Less than nine months," said Curtis. "Under 200 days, if that's what's on your mind."

"998," repeated Edith. "It's a curious number."

"There's something else," said Curtis.

"What?"

"The nightmares are back."

"The same as before?"

He nodded. "Maybe a little worse, even."

"I'm sorry to hear it," said Edith, "But now you must realize that this golden fog of yours is just another manifestation of the problem."

"But I keep seeing it. Two, three, sometimes four times a day."

"And it still doesn't do anything to you?"

"It's terribly cold," he said. "Cold, and malignant."

"That's a supposition, a reaction," said Edith.

"It's there, I tell you!" snapped Curtis. "And it's trying to *become* something."

"What?"

"I don't know, But something. Something evil."

"And the tranquilizers haven't helped?"

"I don't know," he admitted. "I haven't touched them since the first night."

"But why not?"

"They got me too groggy. I was in no condition to defend myself."

"From a fog?"

"From whatever it's going to become."

Edith glanced at her wristwatch. "I'm sorry, Ellery, but I have another appointment in just a minute. Please take those tranquilizers, and we'll speak again the day after tomorrow."

"I'll be back to talk, but I'm not taking those pills."

She shrugged. "As you will. But you're looking very run-down. I wish you could get a good night's sleep."

"So do I," he said grimly.

But he didn't, as he had known he would not. The mist came again, cold and ominous.

He was lying in his bed, pretending to sleep, when he became aware of another presence in the room. He pulled his .38 out from beneath his pillow and fired three quick rounds into the golden mist.

There was no apparent change.

"Damn you!" he yelled, and hurled the gun onto the bed.

The mist moved slowly away from him, hovering just in front of the window, somehow more substantial this time than on any previous occasion. Curtis glared at it for a moment, then aimed a karate blow at its center.

His hand went right through it, and through the window as well. He screamed in pain as a jagged piece of glass caught in the flesh of his forearm, and he withdrew his hand very carefully.

The mist was gone, as he had known it would be, and, dripping blood, he walked to the bathroom in search of gauze or cotton. What he found was a fine mist over the medicine cabinet mirror, and written on it, in the same delicate hand he had seen before, was another number:

997

The next morning he cancelled all his classes for the week. He didn't know exactly what to do, but he was in no condition to teach plump matrons the art of self-defense. He wandered slowly around the city, waiting for the mist to show up again. But it didn't, and he returned home at twilight. Mentally, physically, emotionally exhausted, he grabbed the bannister of the stairs leading to his apartment, and winced as a long lean sliver of wood perforated his hand. Cursing under his breath, he entered the apartment and went to the medicine chest again, and found a new number on a fresh mist:

996

"Is someone trying to drive me crazy, counting down the days I have left?"

"Even assuming that none of this is hallucination, which I do not truthfully assume for a minute," said Edith, "this person must be a very poor mathematician. After all, you went a week from 998 to 997, and only a few hours to 996." She paused, then looked up. "Ellery, I'd like to try a little experiment with you, if I may."

"What kind of experiment?" he said suspiciously.

"I'd like to hypnotize you."

"No! Absolutely not!"

"But it might provide us with a short-cut at getting to the meaning of these numbers."

"I'd make a lousy subject," said Curtis.

"I doubt it," said Edith with a smile. "Hypnosis isn't Barnum and Bailey hocus-pocus any more, Ellery. I can give you a shot of sodium pentothal and—"

"No!"

"But why not?"

"It's out of the question, take my word for it," said Curtis, breaking out in a sweat. "I thought you were supposed to be helping me."

"I'm trying to."

"Then get rid of this demon. Don't dredge up more."

"Whatever do you mean by that?"

"Nothing," he said. "Look, I'm very upset right now. I'd commit myself if I thought it would do the slightest bit of good, would make that damned fog go away. But it won't. That thing is real, and you don't seem to be helping me. I don't know why I keep coming here, except that there aren't any ghost hunters in the phone book. Now, just to humor me, can we assume that I'm really not crazy and that this thing is really following me around?"

"All right," sighed Edith, preparing for a long and fruitless afternoon.

It was there when he got home. He considered attacking it, gave it up as useless, and leaned against his doorway, resigned.

He was aware of a low, indistinct murmuring sound, not at all like the noise of the traffic below him, nor like a radio or television carelessly left on. The fog remained motionless, and he closed his eyes for a moment to concentrate on the murmuring. The sound, like the fog itself, seemed to be trying to take form, to become something tangible. He squeezed his eyes tighter, tried to clear his mind of everything but the murmuring.

And then he heard it, a single word:

*"Griffey."*

He jumped as if he'd stuck his finger in an electric socket.

*"Griffey."*

"Who are you?" he whispered. "What do you want?"

*"Griffey."*

"Go away!" he screamed. "My name is Curtis!"

The word, which had hung on the air, vanished and was replaced by a soundless mirth. Then the fog was gone and he was alone again.

"Ellery Curtis has been dead for almost fifteen years."

"But Ellery..." said Edith.

"Let me finish," he said grimly. "Ellery Curtis was a corporal who had the bad sense to walk into a village before he knew whether it was one of ours or one of theirs. They blew his head off before he knew what hit him."

"But then, who are you?"

"I'm coming to that. About a month later we arrived at the town of Quang Chai, a grubby little place miles from anywhere. The first night we were there, two of our men had their throats slit. We were out of supplies, too sick with fever and jungle rot to march again for days. The village had to be made safe."

"I know," said Edith. "And your commanding officer killed every twentieth man, woman, and child in retaliation while you stood by helplessly. It was terrible, I know, but..."

"They never found him, you know," he said. "He couldn't be brought to trial. Missing in action."

"You don't expect me to believe that this mist is his shade coming back to haunt you for disobeying his order to kill those poor people!" said Edith.

"Hardly," he said. "I wish it was that simple. Would you like to know my real name, Doctor Stillpass?"

"Of course."

He took a deep breath. "James Griffey. Lieutenant James Griffey."

Her mouth dropped open.

"That's right: the Butcher of Quang Chai. Does that help explain the nightmares? I've been running from that godforsaken little nothing in the middle of nowhere for fifteen years. I got rid of the dreams and the headaches, I stopped turning my face away whenever I'd pass a soldier in uniform, I even got to where I could look in the mirror without flinching. And now it's back, and it's not a dream or an hallucination or a guilt complex. It's something else, something real and terrible and malevolent, and it knows who I am and where I live."

Edith was still staring at him unbelievingly. "James Griffey," she repeated tonelessly.

"It was a military decision," he said. "I had no choice!" And with that he walked out of her office.

*"Griffey."*

It was waiting for him on the stairs, and led him up to his apartment.

"Who are you?" he demanded.

*"Griffey."*

"Yes, I'm Griffey, damn you! Now what?"

The golden mist became turbulent, seemed to stiffen and harden, and then underwent a strange and terrible metamorphosis. Slowly, ever so slowly, it formed itself into a hideous golden face, with baleful yellow eyes, brighter than the sun, glaring out.

*"I am Tung Kei Dhu,"* said the face.

"You were at Quang Chai?"

"Yes."

"My job was to protect my men," said Griffey. "I made the right decision, and I'd do it again given the same circumstances."

*"Would you indeed?"*

He nodded defiantly. "If you're here for vengeance, just remember which side began the killing at Quang Chai. I ordered military executions in response to having my men murdered in their sleep."

*"I know why you did what you did,"* said Tung Kei Dhu.

"Then what makes you so moral?" demanded Griffey, trying to hide his desperation. "Who are you to say that killing in retaliation is wrong?"

*"I never said it was wrong. I, too, am an executioner. I bear you no malice for Quang Chai."*

"Then what are you doing here?" demanded Griffey. "Why are you tormenting me?"

*"Listen, James Griffey, and hear me. I am an executioner. My father was an executioner. My grandfather, who lived in China, was an executioner. This was my profession and my life and my art. I was not native to Quang Chai. Do you understand?"*

"So you're an executioner," said Griffey. "So what?"

*"My last commission was to travel to Quang Chai and execute Tien Nhu Po, who had raped and slain my principal's wife and daughter. I bear you no malice for killing me, for such are the fortunes of war."*

"Then why are you here?"

*"Because among the others you killed was Tien Nhu Po."*

"So much the better for you, I should think," said Griffey.

*"Not so. I did not fulfill my commission, and no member of the Family Tung has failed to honor a commission for more than three centuries. I do not blame you for killing Tien Nhu Po, but since he is dead by your hand and not mine, I cannot find eternal peace or rest until I have slain you who slew him."*

"Now that I know who and what you are," said Griffey, measuring his words carefully, "I don't consider it very likely that you're going to scare me to death. Just what is it that you have in mind?"

*"I told you, James Griffey: I am an executioner, not a slaughterer. You must die as Tien Nbu Po was to die."*

"And how was that?"

*"By the Death of a Thousand Cuts."*

"What is that?"

*"The ancient Chinese method of execution. The subject is tied by his wrists to two trees, and the executioner, with consummate art and skill, slashes him one thousand times with his sword. He may peel the skin from the body, he may remove the eyes and ears and limbs, but death cannot come before the thousandth cut."*

Griffey tried to suppress a nervous giggle of relief. "But you have no substance, no solidity. It looks like you're out of luck, Tung Kei Dhu."

*"My task has been made more difficult,"* admitted the huge golden face that shimmered before Griffey, *"but that will only make its accomplishment the more satisfying. The cut on your chin, the glass in your foot, the sliver, the broken window—these were the first four cuts. There are nine hundred ninety-six yet to come."*

"They'll be a long time coming," said Griffey. "I know who and what you are now, and I'll be prepared. I'll sleep with a mask over my eyes, I'll wear earplugs most of the time, I won't be fooled into trying to harm you again. You are going to be one very frustrated spirit, Tung Kei Dhu."

*"We shall see,"* said the face, and vanished.

Nothing unusual happened the next day, or the day after that, and Griffey reopened his martial arts studio. Then, two days after he spoke with the ghost of Tung Kei Dhu, he was walking home just after night fell and decided to cut through an alley to save a little time.

He was no more than fifteen steps into it when he felt a sharp stabbing sensation in his side. He tried to yell, found that his mouth was full of blood, and, gurgling, he fell to the moist pavement. Through a haze of pain he saw three young men kneeling over him, one with a bloody switchblade in his hand. The one with the knife began rifling through Griffey's pockets until he came to his wallet.

"How much?" asked another.

"Shit!" snapped the knife-wielder. "Hardly worth the effort. Nine dollars."

"Try his pockets," said the third man.

"Three quarters and two dimes," announced the first man after a moment.

"A lousy nine ninety-five!" snapped the second.

"Nine ninety-five," repeated the first disgustedly, giving Griffey's head a kick as the three straightened up and raced off into the darkness.

It was only another minute or two before a passerby saw him and called an ambulance. Soon he was on his way to the hospital, but as he was wheeled into the emergency room his mind, hazed over with agony, was far from contemplating his chances of survival.

*Nine ninety-five.*

He awoke as a nurse was injecting something into his forearm.

"What happened?" he said.

"You were mugged and knifed, Mr. Curtis," she replied. "It was a terrible experience, but you've responded very well to treatment."

"Treatment?"

"The blade must have been filthy," said the nurse. "You had a massive infection. We had to do a little surgery."

"My hand hurts," said Griffey.

"Yes. Well, we had a little accident in the operating theater."

"What kind of accident?" he demanded.

"Evidently you weren't anesthesized deeply enough," said the nurse. "Just as surgery was about to begin you swung a wild blow with your right hand.

You didn't hurt anyone, but you did manage to make contact with a scalpel and picked up a rather nasty gash. Took eight stitches to close it up. We strapped you down for the rest of the operation, though you were unconscious again a few seconds later."

"When can I go home?"

"I'm not sure," smiled the nurse. "That's quite a large incision over your wound. On the other hand, you seem to have an iron constitution. Well," she said, "now that you're awake and rational, I'll hunt up the doctor and have him take a look at you. Would you like your door open or closed, Mr. Curtis?"

"Open, if you please," said Griffey.

She walked out, leaving the door open behind her, and Griffey's eyes went wide with horror as he spotted the room number:

994

He spent two weeks in the hospital, and another week recuperating at home. Tung Kei Dhu appeared twice while he was shaving, but he managed to control his reaction and the golden ghost vanished seconds later.

He saw no trace of the fog or the face or anything else associated with Tung Kei Dhu for another month, and had just about convinced himself that the executioner was merely his mind's very strange rationalization for a series of accidents that had befallen him.

There were no more cuts or abrasions, no broken glass, no sleep interrupted by ghostly appearances, no sense of being continually watched. He didn't even worry about his Curtis identity; as horrified as she might be by his past, Edith Stilipass wouldn't break the principle of confidentiality between doctor and patient.

Feeling reasonably good, and totally sane, he decided to treat himself to a good dinner. He was tired of retreating to his apartment night after night and dining on frozen food, and so he walked to one of the better local establishments and ordered a large cut of prime rib of beef. After an appropriate interval the waiter returned with the beef, a baked potato, onion rings, and a steak knife—

—and slipped.

The knife flew four feet through the air, neatly severing his left index finger at the first joint.

He let out a howl of pain, and the restaurant quickly became a scene of pandemonium, everyone running everywhere, tripping over themselves in an effort to help him, or find help for him, or merely gape at him.

Finally a Fire Department ambulance arrived and rushed him off to the hospital. As he got out and walked to the emergency room, the solicitous fireman who had ridden in the back with him laid a gentle hand on his shoulder.

"They've put fingers back on many times," he said gently. "It's probably getting to be old hat to these guys. But if there's anything I can do to help, or you need me to testify in court, just ask for Mikos Papadoupolas."

"I didn't quite catch that name," said Griffey through clenched teeth.

"Nobody can remember it," laughed the fireman. "Just ask for Badge Number 993."

Griffey screamed and fainted.

The next seven months saw a barber inadvertently cut off part of his right earlobe (992), a defective beer can slash his hand open to the bone (991), and a vending machine mirror shatter and rip open his arm while he was waiting for a subway train (990). He also had further surgery on his finger (989) and his knife wound (988).

And there came a day when he knew he could stand it no longer.

His mind made up, he walked out into the middle of an intersection against the light at rush hour, and smiled happily as a huge semi bore down upon him.

And at the last instant a golden mist, no longer transparent, appeared inside the truck's cab. The huge vehicle skidded past him, missing him by less than five feet.

The face of Tung Kei Dhu was waiting for him when he returned home.

*"That was a very foolish thing to do, James Griffey,"* it said. *"You belong to me. No one else may have you."*

"Kill me now or leave me alone!" raged Griffey hysterically. "I can't take any more of this!"

*"Oh, but you can,"* corrected the voice calmly. *"You can take nine hundred eighty-seven more cuts."*

"No!" he screamed. "Please! Please leave me alone!"

*"And if I were to do so, who or what might come after you next, filled with a hate I do not feel? You killed eighty human beings, Butcher of Quang Chai."*

"I'll take my chances!"

*"They are not yours to take, James Griffey,"* said the golden face. *"I am here because I must be here, as are you. Choice is not one of our luxuries."*

Griffey gazed wild-eyed at the face for a moment, then raced to the kitchen. He opened a drawer and pulled out a large butcher knife.

"At least I'll rob you of your revenge!" he yelled, slitting his own throat.

The last words he heard before everything went black were the gentle, emotionless murmurings coming from the now-dissipating golden face: *"I do not act from motives of vengeance, nor will I be robbed."*

Griffey found himself in a gray mist. There was no up or down, no near or far, no points of the compass. There were no seconds or minutes or hours, no hot or cold. There was nothing but Griffey—and one other.

"Welcome, James Griffey."

He turned and found himself confronting a tall, slender, naked Oriental who held an awesome-looking sword in his hand.

"You're Tung Kei Dhu7"

"Your servant," said the man, with a slight bow.

"Where are we7" asked Griffey.

"Elsewhere. Between."

"Between what?"

"Between the last life and the next, James Griffey."

"I don't understand."

"We each have a duty to fulfill, a function to perform, before we pass on to the next plane," said Tung Kei Dhu. "Mine is to apply the Death of a Thousand Cuts to you. Yours is to perish from the thousandth cut."

"But that's crazy!" said Griffey. "I'm already dead. How can you kill me?"

"I don't know," said Tung Kei Dhu, raising the sword high above his head. "But I must try."

The blade came down, slitting Griffey open from Adam's apple to crotch.

The pain was unendurable, yet somehow he endured. He was gutted like a fish, yet he still lived, and slowly, agonizingly, he managed to gather intestines and innards and organs back, to wedge them inside the gaping cavity that used to be his chest and belly. He screamed repeatedly and rasped out his hatred of the swordsman between screams.

"You will heal," said Tung Kei Dhu unemotionally.

Griffey managed to whisper a curse.

"You will heal," continued Tung Kei Dhu calmly, "because you are already dead, as you have pointed out. And yet I must find a way to kill you once more, or I shall never join my ancestors on that higher plane of peace. Yet should I kill you too soon, the disgrace will be no less than should I not kill you at all. We must come down to the Last Cut before I hit upon the solution."

Griffey groaned and tried to vomit, but his internal organs were still too twisted for him to complete the act.

"Farewell, James Griffey," said Tung Kei Dhu, sheathing his sword. "You will heal because you must, and then I shall return."

Griffey watched through glazed eyes as the Oriental walked off into the gray nothingness, becoming as one with the dimensionless mist.

And he knew with an agony that even exceeded the pain of his hideous wounds, that Tung Kei Dhu would indeed be back.

Nine hundred eighty-five more times.

## Introduction to "A Limerick History of Science Fiction"

Back in 1985, I was Guest of Honor at a little convention in New Orleans, and they asked me for a brief piece for their program book. I sat down and, in about 20 minutes I'd knocked off the first version of this poem.

A couple of years later I gave it to George Laskowski to reprint in his Hugo-winning fanzine *Lan's Lantern*.

Then, a decade later, when a semi-prozine called *Pirate Writings* asked me for something, I remembered the poem, pulled it out, fixed the meter a bit, and sold it to them.

So this makes its fourth appearance, which comes to one for every five minutes I worked on it. I wish my books had that kind of track record.

# A LIMERICK HISTORY OF SCIENCE FICTION

## by Mike Wadsworth Resnick

1926 At the start, Hugo brought out *Amazing*,
In spite of some serious hazing
From lawyers and writers.
(It seems that the blighters
Sought cash for their written star-gazing).

1939 John Campbell then surveyed the field,
And said, "Now this drivel must yield.
I shall draw a fine line
With writers like Heinlein,
And think of the power I'll wield!"

1949 Tony Boucher at once saw the light,
And he said (sounding quite erudite):
"I don't give a fig
If the concept is big—
*My* authors must know how to write!"

1950 Then Horace Gold quickly appeared,
And he wasn't the failure we'd feared,
*Galaxy* was afire
With wit and satire—
And the poorer stuff all disappeared.

1964 Then along came Mike Moorcock, who said:
"SF is most certainly dead.
Who wants to re-hash
Even more of this trash?
I'll give them the New Wave instead."

1978 Judy-Lynn del Rey said, "Lester,
Our readers will never dig Bester,

But with cute fuzzy robots
There's no ifs and no buts,
You'll be a most happy investor."

1984 A mirrorshade crowd made the scene,
And said, looking hungry and lean,
"With punks made of cyber,
And no moral fiber,
We'll sweep the bestseller list clean."

1999 When Lucas from college departed,
His vision to film was imparted;
The films have been pleasant,
But quite adolescent—
And now we're right back where we started.

## Introduction to "A Little Knowledge"

This is one of my favorite Kirinyaga stories, because it deals with one of my favorite themes: the choices an artist must make between Facts and Truth.

I was a guest at a convention in France in early 1998, and a woman in the audience asked what I meant. No one had ever asked before, and I answered it rather poorly, saying something about the difference between the dull, mean-spirited, unheroic Wyatt Earp and the legend that has become the truth.

Actually, the proper answer would be this:

Take a loaf of three-month-old bread. The fact is that it's a loaf of moldy bread. But the true visionary sees beyond the mere fact of it, and realizes that it can be penicillin.

That's the crux of the matter, and I tried to give both sides —Koriba and his young apprentice—the best arguments I could muster. Some days I still don't know who's right.

This was a Hugo nominee the same year that "Seven Views of Olduvai Gorge" won the award.

# A LITTLE KNOWLEDGE

There was a time when animals could speak.

Lions and zebras, elephants and leopards, birds and men all shared the earth. They labored side by side, they met and spoke of many things, they exchanged visits and gifts.

Then one day Ngai, who rules the universe from His throne atop Kirinyaga, which men now call Mount Kenya, summoned all of His creations to meet with Him.

"I have done everything I can to make life good for all My creatures," said Ngai. The assembled animals and men began to sing His praises, but Ngai held up His hand, and they immediately stopped.

"I have made life *too* good for you," He continued. "None among you has died for the past year."

"What is wrong with that?" asked the zebra.

"Just as you are constrained by your natures," said Ngai, "just as the elephant cannot fly and the impala cannot climb trees, so I cannot be dishonest. Since no one has died, I cannot feel compassion for you, and without compassion, I cannot water the savannah and the forest with my tears. And without water, the grasses and the trees will shrivel and die."

There was much moaning and wailing from the creatures, but again Ngai silenced them.

"I will tell you a story," He said, "and you must learn from it.

"Once there were two colonies of ants. One colony was very wise, and one colony was very foolish, and they lived next to each other. One day they received word that an aardvark, a creature that eats ants, was coming to their land. The foolish colony went about their business, hoping that the aardvark would ignore them and attack their neighbors. But the wise colony built a mound that could withstand even the efforts of an aardvark, and they gathered sugar and honey, and stockpiled it in the mound.

"When the aardvark reached the kingdom of the ants, he immediately attacked the wise ants, but the mound withstood his greatest efforts, and the ants within survived by eating their sugar and honey. Finally, after many fruitless days, the aardvark wandered over to the kingdom of the foolish ants, and dined well that evening."

Ngai fell silent, and none of His creatures dared ask Him to speak further. Instead, they returned to their homes and discussed His story, and made their preparations for the coming drought.

A year passed, and finally the man decided to sacrifice an innocent goat, and that very day Ngai's tears fell upon the parched and barren land. The next morning Ngai again summoned His creatures to the holy mountain.

"How have you fared during the past year?" He asked each of them.

"Very badly," moaned the elephant, who was very thin and weak. "We did as you instructed us, and built a mound, and gathered sugar and honey—but we grew hot and uncomfortable within the mound, and there is not enough sugar and honey in all the world to feed a family of elephants."

"We have fared even worse," wailed the lion, who was even thinner, "for lions cannot eat sugar and honey at all, but must have meat."

And so it went, as each animal poured out its misery. Finally Ngai turned to the man and ask him the same question.

"We have fared very well," replied the man. "We built a container for water, and filled it before the drought came, and we stockpiled enough grain to last us to this day."

"I am very proud of you," said Ngai. "Of all my creatures, only you understood my story."

"It is not fair!" protested the other animals. "We built mounds and saved sugar and honey, as you told us to!"

"What I told you was a parable," said Ngai, "and you have mistaken the facts of it for the truth that lay beneath. I gave you the power to think, but since you have not used it, I hereby take it away. And as a further punishment, you will no longer have the ability to speak, for creatures that do not think have nothing to say."

And from that day forth, only man, among all Ngai's creations, has had the power to think and speak, for only man can pierce through the facts to find the truth.

★ ★ ★

You think you know a person when you have worked with him and trained him and guided his thinking since he was a small boy. You think you can foresee his reactions to various situations. You think you know how his mind works.

And if the person in question has been chosen by you, selected from the mass of his companions and groomed for something special, as young Ndemi was selected and groomed by me to be my successor as the *mundumugu*—the witch doctor—to our terraformed world of Kirinyaga, the one thing you think above all else is that you possess his loyalty and his gratitude.

But even a *mundumugu* can be wrong.

I do not know exactly when or how it began. I had chosen Ndemi to be my assistant when he was still a *kehee*—an uncircumcized child—and I had worked diligently with him to prepare him for the position he would one day inherit from me. I chose him not for his boldness, though he feared nothing, nor for his enthusiasm, which was boundless, but rather for his intellect, for with the exception of one small girl, long since dead, he was by far the brightest of the children on Kirinyaga. And since we had emigrated to this world to create a Kikuyu paradise, far from the corrupt imitation of Europe that Kenya had become, it was imperative that the *mundumugu* be the wisest of men, for the *mundumugu* not only reads omens and casts spells, but is also the repository for the collected wisdom and culture of his tribe.

Day by day I added to Ndemi's limited storehouse of knowledge. I taught him how to make medicine from the bark and pods of the acacia tree, I showed him how to create the ointments that would ease the discomfort of the aged when the weather turned cold and wet, I made him memorize the hundred spells that were used to bless the scarecrows in the field. I told him a thousand parables, for the Kikuyu have a parable for every need and every occasion, and the wise *mundumugu* is the one who finds the right parable for each situation.

And finally, after he had served me faithfully for six long years, coming up my hill every morning, feeding my chickens and goats, lighting the fire in my *boma*, and filling my empty water gourds before his daily lessons began, I took him into my hut and showed him how my computer worked.

There are only four computers on all of Kirinyaga. The others belong to Koinnage, the paramount chief of our village, and to two chiefs of distant clans, but their computers can do nothing but send and receive messages. Only mine is tied into the data banks of the Eutopian Council, the ruling body that had given Kirinyaga its charter, for only the *mundumugu* has the strength and the vision to be exposed to European culture without becoming corrupted by it.

One of the primary purposes of my computer was to plot the orbital adjustments that would bring seasonal changes to Kirinyaga, so that the rains would come on schedule and the crops would flourish and the harvest would be successful. It was perhaps the *mundumugu's* most important obligation to his people, since it assured their survival. I spent many long days teaching Ndemi all the many intracacies of the computer, until he knew its workings as well as I myself did, and could speak to it with perfect ease.

The morning that I first noticed the change in him began like any other. I awoke, wrapped my blanket around my withered shoulders, and walked painfully out of my hut to sit by my fire until the warming rays of the sun took the chill from the air. And, as always, there was no fire.

Ndemi came up the path to my hill a few minutes later.

"*Jambo* Koriba," he said, greeting me with his usual smile.

"*Jambo*, Ndemi," I said. "How many times have I explained to you that I am an old man, and that I must sit by my fire until the air becomes warmer?"

"I am sorry, Koriba," he said. "But as I was leaving my father's *shamba*, I saw a hyena stalking one of our goats, and I had to drive it off." He held his spear up, as if that were proof of his statement.

I could not help but admire his ingenuity. It was perhaps the thousandth time he had been late, and never had he given the same excuse twice. Still, the situation was becoming intolerable, and when he finished his chores and the fire had warmed my bones and eased my pain, I told him to sit down opposite me.

"What is our lesson for today?" he asked as he squatted down.

"The lesson will come later," I said, finally letting my blanket fall from my shoulders as the first warm breeze of the day blew a fine cloud of dust past my face. "But first I will tell you a story."

He nodded, and stared intently at me as I began speaking.

"Once there was a Kikuyu chief," I said. "He had many admirable qualities. He was a mighty warrior, and in council his words carried great weight. But along with his many good qualities, he also had a flaw.

"One day he saw a maiden tilling the fields in her father's *shamba*, and he was smitten with her. He meant to tell her of his love the very next day, but as he set out to see her, his way was blocked by an elephant, and he retreated and waited until the elephant had passed. When he finally arrived at the maiden's *boma*, he discovered that a young warrior was paying her court. Nevertheless, she smiled at him when their eyes met, and, undiscouraged, he made up his mind to visit her the following day. This time a deadly snake blocked his way, and once again, when he arrived he found the maiden being courted by his rival. Once more she gave him an encouraging smile, and so he decided to come back a third time.

"On the morning of the third day, he lay on his blanket in his hut, and thought about all the many things he wanted to tell her to impress her with his ardor. By the time he had decided upon the best approach to win her favor, the sun was setting. He ran all the way from his *boma* to that of the maiden, only to find that his rival had just paid her father five cattle and thirty goats for her hand in marriage.

"He managed to get the maiden alone for a moment, and poured forth his litany of love.

"'I love you too,' she answered, 'but although I waited for you each day, and hoped that you would come, you were always late.'

"'I have excuses to offer,' he said. 'On the first day I encountered an elephant, and on the second day a killer snake was in my path.' He did not dare tell her the real reason he was late a third time, so he said, 'And today a leopard confronted me, and I had to kill it with my spear before I could continue on my way.'

"'I am sorry,' said the maiden, 'but I am still promised to another.'

"'Do you not believe me?' he demanded.

"'It makes no difference whether you are telling the truth or not,' she replied. 'For whether the lion and the snake and the leopard are real or whether they are lies, the result is the same: you have lost your heart's desire because you were late.'"

I stopped and stared at Ndemi. "Do you understand the moral of my story?" I asked.

He nodded. "It does not matter to you whether a hyena was stalking my father's goat or not. All that matters is that I was late."

"That is correct," I said.

This is where such things had always ended, and then we would begin his lessons. But not this day.

"It is a foolish story," he said, looking out across the vast savannah.

"Oh?" I asked. "Why?"

"Because it begins with a lie."

"What lie?"

"The Kikuyu had no chiefs until the British created them," he answered.

"Who told you that?" I asked.

"I learned it from the box that glows with life," he said, finally meeting my gaze.

"My computer?"

He nodded again. "I have had many long discussions about the Kikuyu with it, and I have learned many things." He paused. "We did not even live in villages until the time of the Mau Mau, and then the British *made* us live together so that we could be more easily watched. And it was the British who created our tribal chiefs, so that they could rule us through them."

"That is true," I acknowledged. "But it is unimportant to my story."

"But your story was untrue with its first line," he said, "so why should the rest of it be true? Why did you not just say, 'Ndemi, if you are late again, I will not care whether your reason is true or false. I will punish you.'"

"Because it is important for you to understand *why* you must not be late."

"But the story is a lie. Everyone knows that it takes more than three days to court and purchase a wife. So it began with a lie and it ended with a lie."

"You are looking at the surface of things," I said, watching a small insect crawl over my foot and finally flicking it off. "The truth lies beneath."

"The truth is that you do not want me to be late. What has that to do with the elephant and the leopard, which were extinct before we came to Kirinyaga?"

"Listen to me, Ndemi," I said. "When you become the *mundumugu*, you will have to impart certain values, certain lessons, to your people—and you must do so in a way that they understand. This is especially true of the children, who are the clay that you will mold into the next generation of Kikuyu."

Ndemi was silent for a long moment. "I think you are wrong, Koriba," he said at last. "Not only will the people understand you if you speak plainly to them, but stories like the one you just told me are filled with lies which they will think are true simply because they come from the *mundumugu's* lips."

*"No!"* I said sharply. "We came to Kirinyaga to live as the Kikuyu lived before the Europeans tried to change us into that characterless tribe known as Kenyans. There is a poetry to my stories, a tradition to them. They reach out to our racial memory of the way things were, and the way we hope to make them again." I paused to consider which path to follow, for never before had Ndemi so bluntly opposed my teachings. "You yourself used to beg me for stories, and of all the children you were the quickest to find the true meaning of them."

"I was younger then," he said.

"You were a Kikuyu then," I said.

"I am still a Kikuyu."

"You are a Kikuyu who has been exposed to European knowledge and European history," I said. "This is unavoidable, if you are to succeed me as the *mundumugu*, for we hold our charter at the whim of the Europeans, and you must be able to speak to them and work their machine. But your greatest challenge, as a Kikuyu and a *mundumugu*, is to avoid becoming corrupted by them."

"I do not *feel* corrupted," he said. "I have learned many things from the computer."

"So you have," I agreed, as a fish eagle circled lazily overhead and the breeze brought the smell of a nearby herd of wildebeest. "And you have forgotten many things."

"What have I forgotten?" he demanded, watching the fish eagle swoop down and grab a fish from the river. "You may test me and see how good my memory is."

"You have forgotten that the true value of a story is that the listener must bring something to it," I said. "I could simply order you not to be late, as you suggest—but the purpose of the story is to make you use your brain to understand *why* you should not be late." I paused. "You are also forgetting that the reason we do not try to become like the Europeans is because we tried once before, and became only Kenyans."

He was silent for a long time. Finally he looked up at me.

"May we skip today's lesson?" he asked. "You have given me much to think about."

I nodded my acquiesence. "Come back tomorrow, and we will discuss your thoughts."

He stood up and walked down the long winding path that led from my hill to the village.

But though I waited for him until the sun was high in the sky the next day, he did not come back.

Just as it is good for fledgling birds to test their wings, it is good for young people to test *their* powers by questioning authority. I bore Ndemi no malice, but simply waited until the day that he returned, somewhat humbled, to resume his studies.

But the fact that I now had no assistant did not absolve me of my duties, and so each day I walked down to the village, and blessed the scarecrows, and took my place alongside Koinnage in the Council of Elders. I brought new ointment for old Siboki's joints, which were causing him discomfort, and I sacrificed a goat so that Ngai would look with favor upon the pending marriage of Maruta with a man of another clan.

As always, when I made my rounds, I was followed everywhere by the village children, who begged me to stop what I was doing and tell them a story. For two days I was too busy, for a *mundumugu* has many tasks to perform, but on the morning of the third day I had some time to spare, and I gathered them around me in the shade of an acacia tree.

"What kind of story would you like to hear?" I asked.

"Tell us of the old days, when we still lived in Kenya," said a girl.

I smiled. They always asked for stories of Kenya—not that they knew where Kenya was, or what it meant to the Kikuyu. But when we lived in Kenya the lion and the rhinoceros and the elephant were not yet extinct, and they loved stories in which animals spoke and displayed greater wisdom than men, a wisdom that they themselves assimilated as I repeated the stories.

"Very well," I said. "I will tell you the story of the Foolish Lion."

They all sat or squatted down in a semi-circle, facing me with rapt attention, and I continued: "Once there was a foolish lion who lived on the slopes of Kirinyaga, the holy mountain, and because he was a foolish lion, he did not believe that Ngai had given the mountain to Gikuyu, the very first man. Then one morning..."

"That is wrong, Koriba," said one of the boys.

I focused my weak eyes on him, and saw that it was Mdutu, the son of Karenja.

"You have interrupted your *mundumugu*," I noted harshly. "And, even worse, you have contradicted him. Why?"

"Ngai did not give Kirinyaga to Gikuyu," said Mdutu, getting to his feet.

"He most certainly did," I replied. "Kirinyaga belongs to the Kikuyu."

"That cannot be so," he persisted, "for Kirinyaga is not a Kikuyu name, but a Maasai name. *Kiri* means *mountain* in the language of Maa, and *nyaga* means *light*. Is it not more likely that Ngai gave the mountain to the Maasai, and that our warriors took it away from them?"

"How do you know what these words mean in the language of the Maasai?" I demanded. "That language is not known to anyone on Kirinyaga."

"Ndemi told us," said Mdutu.

"Well, Ndemi is wrong!" I shouted. "The truth has been passed on from Gikuyu through his nine daughters and his nine sons-in-law all the way down to me, and never has it varied. The Kikuyu are Ngai's chosen people. Just as He gave the spear and Kilimanjaro to the Maasai, He gave the digging-stick and Kirinyaga to us. Kirinyaga has always belonged to the Kikuyu, and it always will!"

"No, Koriba, you are wrong," said a soft, high-pitched voice, and I turned to face my new assailant. It was tiny Thimi, the daughter of Njomu, barely seven years old, who rose to contradict me.

"Ndemi told us that many years ago the Kikuyu sold Kirinyaga to a European named John Boyes for six goats, and it was the British government that made him return it to us."

"Who do you believe?" I demanded severely. "A young boy who has lived for only fifteen long rains, or your *mundumugu*?"

"I do not know," she answered with no sign of fear. "He tells us dates and places, and you speak of wise elephants and foolish lions. It is very hard to decide."

"Then perhaps instead of the story of the Foolish Lion," I said, "I will tell you the story of the Arrogant Boy."

"No, no, the lion!" shouted some of the children.

"Be quiet!" I snapped. "You will hear what *I* want to tell you!"

Their protests subsided, and Thimi sat down again.

"Once there was a bright young boy," I began.

"Was his name Ndemi?" asked Mdutu with a smile.

"His name was Legion," I answered. "Do not interrupt again, or I shall leave and there will be no more stories until the next rains."

The smile vanished from Mdutu's face, and he lowered his head.

"As I said, this was a very bright boy, and he worked on his father's *shamba*, herding the goats and cattle. And because he was a bright young boy, he was always thinking, and one day he thought of a way to make his chores easier. So he went to his father and said that he had had a dream, and in this dream they had built a wire enclosure with sharp barbs on the wire, to keep the cattle in and the hyenas out, and he was sure that if he were to build such an enclosure, he would no longer have to herd the cattle but would be free to do other things.

"'I am glad to see that you are using your brain,' said the boy's father, 'but that idea has been tried before, by the Europeans. If you wish to free yourself from your duties, you must think of some other way.'

"'But why?' said the boy. 'Just because the Europeans thought of it does not make it bad. After all, it must work for *them* or they would not use it.'

"'That is true,' said his father. 'But what works for the Europeans does not necessarily work for the Kikuyu. Now do your chores, and keep thinking, and if you think hard enough I am sure you will come up with a better idea.'

"But along with being bright, the boy was also arrogant, and he refused to listen to his father, even though his father was older and wiser and more experienced. So he spent all his spare time attaching sharp little barbs to the wire, and when he was done he built an enclosure and put his father's cattle into it, sure that they could not get out and the hyenas could not find a way in. And when the enclosure was completed, he went to sleep for the night."

I paused and surveyed my audience. Most of them were staring raptly at me, trying to figure out what came next.

"He awoke to screams of anger from his father and wails of anguish from his mother and sisters, and ran out to see what had happened. He found all of his father's cattle dead. During the night the hyenas, whose jaws can crush a bone, had bitten through the posts to which the wire was attached, and the cattle, in their panic, ran into the wire and were held motionless by the barbs while the hyenas killed and ate them.

"The arrogant boy looked upon the carnage with puzzlement. 'How can this have happened?' he said. 'The Europeans have used this wire, and it never happened to them.'

"'There are no hyenas in Europe,' said his father. 'I told you that we are different from the Europeans, and that what works for them will not work for us, but you refused to listen, and now we must live our lives in poverty, for in a single night your arrogance cost me the cattle that it has taken me a lifetime to accumulate.'"

I fell silent and waited for a response.

"Is that all?" asked Mdutu at last.

"That is all."

"What did it mean?" asked another of the boys.

"You tell *me*," I said.

Nobody answered for a few moments. Then Balimi, Thimi's older sister, stood up.

"It means that only Europeans can use wire with barbs on it."

"No," I said. "You must not only listen, child, but *think*."

"It means that what works for the Europeans will not work for the Kikuyu," said Mdutu, "and that it is arrogant to believe that it will."

"That is correct," I said.

"That is *not* correct," said a familiar voice from behind me, and I turned to see Ndemi standing there. "All it means is that the boy was too foolish to cover the posts with the wire."

The children looked at him, and began nodding their heads in agreement.

"No!" I said firmly. "It means that we must reject all things European, including their ideas, for they were not meant for the Kikuyu."

"But why, Koriba?" asked Mdutu. "What is wrong with what Ndemi says?"

"Ndemi tells you only the facts of things," I said. "But because he, too, is an arrogant boy, he fails to see the truth."

"What truth does he fail to see?" persisted Mdutu.

"That if the wire enclosure were to work, then the next day the arrogant boy would borrow another idea from the Europeans, and yet another, until he had no Kikuyu ideas left, and he had turned his *shamba* into a European farm."

"Europe is an exporter of food," said Ndemi. "Kenya is an importer."

"What does that mean?" asked Thimi.

"It means that Ndemi has a little knowledge, and does not yet know that that is a dangerous thing," I answered.

"It means," responded Ndemi, "that European farms produce more than enough to feed their tribes, and Kenyan farms do not produce enough. And if that is the case, it means that some European ideas may be good for the Kikuyu."

"Perhaps you should wear shoes like the Europeans," I said angrily, "since you have decided to become one."

He shook his head. "I am a Kikuyu, not a European. But I do not wish to be an ignorant Kikuyu. How can we remain true to what we were, when your fables hide what we were from us?"

"No," I said. "They *reveal* it."

"I am sorry, Koriba," said Ndemi, "for you are a great *mundumugu* and I respect you above all men, but in this matter you are wrong." He paused and stared at me. "Why did you never tell us that the only time in our history the Kikuyu were united under the leadership of a single king, the king was a white man named John Boyes?"

The children gasped in amazement.

"If we do not know how it happened," continued Ndemi, "how can we prevent it from happening again? You tell us stories of our wars with the Maasai, and they are wonderful tales of courage and victory—but according to the computer, we lost every war we ever fought against them. Shouldn't we know that, so if the Maasai ever come to Kirinyaga, we are not deluded into fighting them because of the fables we have heard?"

"Koriba, is that true?" asked Mdutu. "Was our only king a European?"

"Did we never defeat the Maasai?" asked another of the children.

"Leave us for a moment," I said, "and then I will answer you."

The children reluctantly got up and walked away until they were out of earshot, then stood and stared at Ndemi and myself.

"Why have you done this?" I said to Ndemi. "You will destroy their pride in being Kikuyu!"

"I am not less proud for knowing the truth," said Ndemi. "Why should they be?"

"The stories I tell them are designed to make them distrust European ways, and to make them happy they are Kikuyu," I explained, trying to control my temper. "You will undermine the confidence they must have if Kirinyaga is to remain our Utopia."

"Most of us have never even seen a European," answered Ndemi. "When I was younger, I used to dream about them, and in my dreams they had claws like a lion and shook the earth like an elephant when they walked. How does that prepare us for the day that we actually meet with them?"

"You will never meet them on Kirinyaga," I said. "And the purpose of my stories is to *keep* us on Kirinyaga." I paused. "Once before we had never seen Europeans, and we were so taken by their machines and their medicines and their religions that we tried to become Europeans ourselves, and succeeded only in becoming something other than Kikuyu. That must never happen again."

"But isn't it less likely to happen if you tell the children the truth?" persisted Ndemi.

"I *do* tell them the truth!" I said. "It is *you* who are confusing them with facts—facts that you got from European historians and a European computer."

"Are the facts wrong?"

"That is not the issue, Ndemi," I said. "These are *children*. They must learn as children do—as you yourself did."

"And after their circumcision rituals, when they become adults, will you tell them the facts then?"

That sentence was as close to rebellion as he had ever come —indeed, as *anyone* on Kirinyaga had ever come. Never had I been more fond of a young man than I was of Ndemi—not even of my own son, who had chosen to remain in Kenya. Ndemi was bright, he was bold, and it was hardly unusual for one of his age to question authority. Therefore, I decided to make another attempt to reason to him, rather than risk a permanent rift in our relationship.

"You are still the brightest young man on Kirinyaga," I said truthfully, "so I will pose you a question, and I will expect an honest answer. You seek after history, and I seek after truth. Which do you suppose is the more important?"

He frowned. "They are the same," he answered. "History *is* truth."

"No," I replied. "History is a compilation of facts and events, which is subject to constant reinterpretation. It begins with truth, and evolves into fable. My stories begin with fable and evolve into truth."

"If you are right," he said thoughtfully, "then your stories are more important than history."

"Very well, then," I said, hoping that the matter was closed.

"But," he added, "I am not sure that you are right. I will have to think more about it."

"Do that," I said. "You are an intelligent boy. You will come to the right conclusion."

Ndemi turned and began walking off in the direction of his family's *shamba.* The children rushed back as soon as he was out of sight, and once more squatted in a tight semi-circle.

"Have you an answer to my question, Koriba?" asked Mdutu.

"I cannot recall your question," I said.

"Was our only king a white man?"

"Yes."

"How could that be?"

I considered my response for a long moment.

"I will answer that by telling you the story of the little Kikuyu girl who became, very briefly, the queen of all the elephants," I said.

"What has that to do with the white man who became our king?" persisted Mdutu.

"Listen carefully," I instructed him, "for when I am done, I shall ask you many questions about my story, and before we are through, you will have the answer to your own question."

He leaned forward attentively, and I began reciting my fable.

I returned to my *boma* to take the noon meal. After I had finished it, I decided to take a nap during the heat of the day, for I am an old man and it had been a long, wearing morning. I let my goats and chickens loose on my hillside, secure in the knowledge that no one would take them away since they each carried the *mundumugu's* mark. I had just spread my sleeping blanket out beneath the branches of my acacia tree when I saw two figures at the foot of my hill.

At first I thought they were two village boys, looking for cattle that had strayed from their pastures, but when the figures began walking up the slopes of my hill I was finally able to focus my eyes on them. The larger figure was Shima, Ndemi's mother, and the smaller was a goat that she led by a rope that she had tied around its neck.

Finally she reached my *boma*, somewhat out of breath, for the goat was unused to the rope and constantly pulled against it, and opened the gate.

"*Jambo*, Shima," I said, as she entered the *boma*. "Why have you brought your goat to my hill? You know that only my own goats may graze here."

"It is a gift for you, Koriba," she replied.

"For me?" I said. "But I have done you no service in exchange for it."

"You can, though. You can take Ndemi back. He is a good boy, Koriba."

"But—"

"He will never be late again," she promised. "He truly did save our goat from a hyena. He would never lie to his *mundumugu*. He is young, but he can become a great *mundumugu* someday. I know he can, if you will just teach him. You are a wise man, Koriba, and you have made a wise choice in Ndemi. I do not know why you have banished him, but if you will just take him back he will never misbehave again. He wants only to become a great *mundumugu* like yourself. Though of course," she added hastily, "he could never be as great as you."

"Will finally you let me speak?" I asked irritably.

"Certainly, Koriba."

"I did not cast Ndemi out. He left of his own volition."

Her eyes widened. "*He* left *you*?"

"He is young, and rebellion is part of youth."

"So is foolishness!" she exclaimed furiously. "He has *always* been foolish. *And* late! He was even two weeks late being born when I carried him! He is always thinking, instead of doing his chores. For the longest time I thought we had been cursed, but then you made him your assistant, and I was to become the mother of the *mundumugu*, and now he has ruined everything!"

She let go of the rope, and the goat wandered around my *boma* as she began beating her breasts with her fists.

"Why am *I* so cursed?" she demanded. "Why does Ngai give me a fool for a son, and then stir my hopes by sending him to you, and then curse me doubly by returning him, almost a man and unable to perform any of the chores on our *shamba*? What will become of him? Who will accept a bride-price from such a fool? He will be late to plant our seed and late to harvest it, he will be late to choose a bride and late to make the payment on her, and he will end up living with the unmarried men at the edge of the forest and begging for food. With my luck he will even be late to die!" She paused for breath, then began wailing again, and finally screamed: "Why does Ngai hate me so?"

"Calm yourself, Shima," I said.

"It is easy for *you* to say!" she sobbed. "You have not lost all hope for your future."

"My future is of very limited duration," I said. "It is Kirinyaga's future that concerns me."

"See?" she said, wailing and beating her breasts again. "See? I am the mother of the boy who will destroy Kirinyaga!"

"I did not say that."

"What has he done, Koriba?" she said. "Tell me, and I will have his father and brothers beat him until he behaves."

"Beating him is not the solution," I said. "He is young, and he rebels against my authority. It is the way of things. Before long he will realize that he is wrong."

"I will explain to him all that he can lose, and he will know that he should never disagree with you, and he will come back."

"You might suggest it," I encouraged her. "I am an old man, and I have much left to teach him."

"I will do as you say, Koriba," she promised.

"Good," I said. "Now go back to your *shamba* and speak to Ndemi, for I have other things to do."

It was not until I awoke from my nap and returned to the village to sit at the Council of Elders that I realized just how many things I had to do.

Our daily business is always conducted in late afternoon, when the heat of the day has passed, at the *boma* of Koinnage, the paramount chief. One by one the Elders place their mats in a semi-circle and sit on them, with my place being at Koinnage's right hand. The *boma* is cleared of all women, children, and animals, and when the last of us has arrived, Koinnage calls us into session. He announces what problems are to be considered, and then I ask Ngai to guide our judgment and allow us to come to just decisions.

On this particular day, two of the villagers had asked the Council of Elders to determine the ownership of a calf that was born to a cow they jointly owned; Sebana wanted permission to divorce his youngest wife, who had now been barren for three years; and Kijo's three sons were unhappy with the way his estate had been divided among them.

Koinnage consulted with me in low whispers after each petition had been heard, and took my advice, as always. The calf went to the man who had fed the cow during her pregnancy, with the understanding that the other man should own the next calf. Sebana was told that he could divorce his wife, but would not receive the bride price back, and he elected to keep her. Kijo's sons were told that they could accept the division as it was, or if two of them agreed, I would place three colored stones in a gourd, and they could each withdraw a stone and own the *shamba* that it represented. Since each faced the possibility of ending up with the smallest *shamba*, only one brother voted for our solution, as I had foreseen, and the petition was dismissed.

At this point, Koinnage's senior wife, Wambu, would usually appear with a large gourd of *pombe*, and we would drink it and then return to our *bomas*, but this day Wambu did not come, and Koinnage turned nervously to me.

"There is one thing more, Koriba," he said.

"Oh?"

He nodded, and I could see the muscles in his face tensing as he worked up the courage to confront his *mundumugu*.

"You have told us that Ngai handed the burning spear to Jomo Kenyatta, that he might create Mau Mau and drive the Europeans from Kenya."

"That is true," I said.

"Is it?" he replied. "I have been told that he himself married a European woman, that Mau Mau did *not* succeed in driving the Europeans from the holy mountain, and that Jomo Kenyatta was not even his real name—that he was actually born with the European name Johnstone." He stared at me, half-accusing, half-terrified of arousing my wrath. "What have you to say to this, Koriba?"

I met his gaze and held it for a long time, until he finally dropped his eyes. Then, one by one, I looked coldly at each member of the Council.

"So you prefer to believe a foolish young boy to your own *mundumugu*?" I demanded.

"We do not believe the boy, but the computer," said Karenja.

"And have you spoken to the computer yourselves?"

"No," said Koinnage. "That is another thing we must discuss. Ndemi tells me that your computer speaks to him and tells him many things, while *my* computer can do nothing but send messages to the other chiefs."

"It is a *mundumugu's* tool, not to be used by other men," I replied.

"Why?" asked Karenja. "It knows many things that we do not know. We could learn much from it."

"You *have* learned much from it," I said. "It speaks to me, and I speak to you."

"But it also speaks to Ndemi," continued Karenja, "and if it can speak to a boy barely past circumcision age, why can it not speak directly to the Elders of the village?"

I turned to Karenja and held my two hands in front of me, palms up. "In my left hand is the meat of an impala that I killed today," I said. "In my right is the meat of an impala that I killed five days ago and left to sit in the sun. It is covered with ants, worms crawl through it, and it stinks." I paused. "Which of the two pieces of meat will you eat?"

"The meat in your left hand," he answered.

"But both pieces of meat came from the same herd of impala," I pointed out. "Both animals were equally fat and healthy when they died."

"But the meat in your right hand is rotten," he said.

"That is true," I agreed. "And just as there can be good and bad meat, so there can be good and bad facts. The facts Ndemi has related to you come from books written by the Europeans, and facts can mean different things to them than they mean to us."

I paused while they considered what I had said, and then continued. "A European may look upon the savannah and envision a city, while a Kikuyu may look at the same savannah and see a *shamba*. A European may look at an elephant and see ivory trinkets, while a Kikuyu may look at the same elephant and see food for his village, or destruction for his crops. And yet they are looking at the same land, and the same animal.

"Now," I said, once again looking at each of them in turn, "I have been to school in Europe, and in America, and only I, of all the men and women on Kirinyaga, have lived among the white man. And I tell you that only I, your *mundumugu*, am capable of separating the good facts from the bad facts. It was a mistake to allow Ndemi to speak with my computer; I will not allow it again, until I have given him more of my wisdom."

I had thought my statement would put an end to the matter, but as I looked around I saw signs of discomfort, as if they wished to argue with me but lacked the courage. Finally Koinnage leaned forward and, without looking directly at me, said, "Do you not see what you are saying, Koriba? If the *mundumugu* can make a mistake by allowing a young boy to speak with his computer, can he not also make a mistake by not allowing the Elders to speak to it?"

I shook my head. "It is a mistake to allow *any* Kikuyu except the *mundumugu* to speak to it."

"But there is much that we can learn from it," persisted Koinnage.

"What?" I asked bluntly.

He shrugged helplessly. "If I knew, then I would already have learned it."

"How many times must I repeat this to you: there is nothing to be learned from the Europeans. The more you try to become like them, the less you remain Kikuyu. This is *our* Utopia, a *Kikuyu* Utopia. We must fight to preserve it."

"And yet," said Karenja, "even the word Utopia is European, is it not?"

"You heard that from Ndemi, too?" I asked without hiding the annoyance from my voice.

He nodded his head. "Yes."

"Utopia is just a word," I said. "It is the *idea* that counts."

"If the Kikuyu have no word for it and the Europeans do, perhaps it is a European idea," said Karenja. "And if we have built our world upon a European idea, perhaps there are other European ideas that we can also use."

I looked at their faces, and realized, for perhaps the first time, that most of the original Elders of Kirinyaga had died. Old Siboki remained, and I could tell by his face that he found European ideas even more abhorrent than I myself did, and there were two or three others, but this was a new generation of Elders, men who had come to maturity on Kirinyaga and could not remember the reasons we had fought so hard to come here.

"If you want to become black Europeans, go back to Kenya!" I snapped in disgust. "It is filled with them!"

"We are not black Europeans," said Karenja, refusing to let the matter drop. "We are Kikuyu who think it is possible that not all European ideas are harmful."

"Any idea that changes us is harmful," I said.

"Why?" asked Koinnage, his courage to oppose me growing as he realized that many of the Elders supported him. "Where is it written that a Utopia cannot grow and change? If that were the case, we would have ceased to be a Utopia the day the first baby was born on Kirinyaga."

"There are as many Utopias as there are races," I said. "None among you would argue that a Kikuyu Utopia is the same as a Maasai Utopia or a Samburu Utopia. By the same token, a Kikuyu Utopia cannot be a European Utopia. The closer you come to the one, the farther you move from the other."

They had no answer to that, and I got to my feet.

"I am your *mundumugu*," I said. "I have never misled you. You have always trusted my judgment in the past. You must trust in it in this instance."

As I began walking out of the *boma*, I heard Karenja's voice behind me.

"If you were to die tomorrow, Ndemi would become our *mundumugu*. Are you saying we should trust his judgment as we trust yours?"

I turned to face him. "Ndemi is very young and inexperienced. You, as the Elders of the village, would have to use your wisdom to decide whether or not what he says is correct."

"A bird that has been caged all its life cannot fly," said Karenja, "just as a flower that has been kept from the sun will not blossom."

"What is your point?" I asked.

"Shouldn't we begin using our wisdom now, lest we forget how when Ndemi has become the *mundumugu*?"

This time it was I who had no answer, so I turned on my heel and began the long walk back to my hill.

For five days I fetched my own water and made my own fires, and then Ndemi returned, as I had known he would.

I was sitting in my *boma*, idly watching a herd of gazelles grazing across the river, when he trudged up the path to my hill, looking distinctly uncomfortable.

"*Jambo*, Ndemi," I said. "It is good to see you again."

"*Jambo*, Koriba," he replied.

"And how was your vacation?" I asked, but there is no Swahili word for *vacation* so I used the English term and the humor and sarcasm were lost on him.

"My father urged me to come back," he said, bending over to pet one of my goats, and I saw the welts on his back that constituted his 'urging'.

"I am glad to have you back, Ndemi," I said. "We have become like father and son, and it pains me when we argue, as I am sure it pains you."

"It *does* pain me," he admitted. "I do not like to disagree with you, Koriba."

"We have both made mistakes," I continued. "You argued with your *mundumugu*, and I allowed you access to all that information before you were mature enough to know what to do with it. We are both intelligent enough to learn from our mistakes. You are still my chosen successor. It shall be as if it never happened."

"But it *did* happen, Koriba," he said.

"We shall pretend it did not."

"I do not think I can do that," said Ndemi unhappily, protecting his eyes as a sudden wind blew dust across the *boma*. "I learned many things when I spoke to the computer. How can I unlearn them?"

"If you cannot unlearn them, then you will have to ignore them until you are older," I said. "*I* am your teacher. The computer is just a tool. You will use it to bring the rains, and to send an occasional message to Maintenance, and that is all."

A black kite swooped down and made off with a scrap of my morning meal that had fallen beside the embers of my fire. I watched it while I waited for Ndemi to speak.

"You appear troubled," I said, when it became apparent that he would not speak first. "Tell me what bothers you."

"It was you who taught me to think, Koriba," he said as various emotions played across his handsome young face. "Would you have me stop thinking now, just because I think differently than you do?"

"Of course I do not want you to stop thinking, Ndemi," I said, not without sympathy, for I understood the forces at war within him. "What good would a *mundumugu* be if he could not think? But just as there are right and wrong ways to throw a spear, there are right and wrong ways to think. I wish only to see you take the path of true wisdom."

"It will be greater wisdom if I come upon it myself," he said. "I must learn as many facts as I can, so that I can properly decide which are helpful and which are harmful."

"You are still too young," I said. "You must trust me until you are older, and better able to make those decisions."

"The facts will not change."

"No, but *you* will."

"But how can I know that change is for the good?" he asked. "What if you are wrong, and by listening to you until I become like you, I will be wrong too?"

"If you think I am wrong, why have you come back?"

"To listen, and decide," he said. "And to speak to the computer again."

"I cannot permit that," I said. "You have already caused great mischief among the tribe. Because of you, they are questioning everything I say."

"There is a reason for that."

"Perhaps you will tell me what it is?" I said, trying to keep the sarcasm from my voice, for I truly loved this boy and wished to win him back to my side.

"I have listened to your stories for many years now, Koriba," he said, "and I believe that I can use *your* method to show you the reason."

I nodded my head and waited for him to continue.

"This should be called the story of Ndemi," he said, "but because I am pretending to be Koriba, I shall call it the story of the Unborn Lion."

I plucked an insect from my cheek and rolled it between my fingers until the carapace cracked. "I am listening."

"Once there was an unborn lion who was very anxious to see the world," began Ndemi. "He spent much time talking about it to his unborn brothers. 'The world will be a wonderful place,' he assured them. 'The sun will always be shining, and the plains will be filled with fat, lazy impala, and all other animals will bow before us, for there shall be no animal mightier than us.'

"His brothers urged him to stay where he was. 'Why are you so anxious to be born?' they asked him. 'Here it is warm and safe, and we never hunger. Who knows what awaits us in the world?'

"But the unborn lion would hear none of it, and one night, while his mother and brethren slept, he stole out into the world. He could not see, so he nudged his mother and said, 'Where is the sun?' and she told him that the sun vanishes every evening, leaving the world cold and dark. 'At least when it comes back tomorrow, it will shine on fat lazy impala that we will catch and eat,' he said, trying to console himself.

"But his mother said, 'There are no impala here, for they have migrated with the rains to the far side of the world. All that is left for us to eat is the buffalo. Their flesh is tough and tasteless, and they kill as many of us as we kill of them.'

"'If my stomach is empty, at least my spirit will be full,' said the newly-born lion, 'for all other animals will look upon us with fear and envy.'

"'You are very foolish, even for a newly-born cub,' said his mother. "'The leopard and the hyena and the eagle look upon you not as an object of envy, but rather as a tasty meal.'

"'At least all of them will fear me when I am fully grown,' said the newly-born lion.

"'The rhinoceros will gore you with his horn,' said his mother, 'and the elephant will toss you high into the trees with his trunk. Even the black mamba will not step aside for you, and will kill you if you try to approach it.'

"The mother continued her list of all the animals that would neither fear nor envy the lion when he grew up, and finally he told her to speak no more.

"'I have made a terrible mistake by being born,' he said. 'The world is not as I pictured it, and I will rejoin my brothers where they are warm and safe and comfortable.

"But his mother merely smiled at him. 'Oh, no,' she said, not without compassion. 'Once you are born, whether it is of your own choosing or mine, you cannot ever go back to being an unborn lion. Here you are, and here you shall stay.'"

Ndemi looked at me, his story finished.

"It is a very wise story," I said. "I could not have done better myself. I knew the day I first made you my pupil that you would make a fine *mundumugu*."

"You still do not understand," he said unhappily.

"I understand the story perfectly," I replied.

"But it is a lie," said Ndemi. "I told it only to show you how easy it is to make up such lies."

"It is not easy at all," I corrected him. "It is an art, mastered only by a few—and now that I see that you have mastered it, it would be doubly hurtful to lose you."

"Art or not, it is a lie," he repeated. "If a child heard and believed it, he would be sure that lions could speak, and that babies can be born whenever they chose to be." He paused. "It would have been much simpler to tell you that once I have obtained knowledge, whether is was freely given or not, I cannot empty my mind and give it back. Lions have nothing to do with that." He paused for a long moment. "Furthermore, I do not *want* to give my knowledge back. I want to learn more things, not forget those that I already know."

"You must not say that, Ndemi," I urged him. "Especially now that I see that my teachings have taken root, and that your abilities as a creator of fables will someday surpass my own. You can be a great *mundumugu* if you will just allow me to guide you."

"I love and respect you as I do my own father, Koriba," he replied. "I have always listened and tried to learn from you, and I will continue to do so for as long as you will permit me. But you are not the only source of knowledge. I also wish to learn what your computer can teach me."

"When I decide you are ready."

"I am ready now."

"You are not."

His face reflected an enormous inner battle, and I could only watch until it was resolved. Finally he took a deep breath and let it out slowly.

"I am sorry, Koriba, but I cannot continue to tell lies when there are truths to be learned." He laid a hand on my shoulder. "*Kwaheri, mwalimu.*" *Good-bye, my teacher.*

"What will you do?"

"I cannot work on my father's *shamba*," he said, "not after all that I have learned. Nor do I wish to live in isolation with the bachelors at the edge of the forest."

"What is left for you?" I asked.

"I shall walk to that area of Kirinyaga called Haven, and await the next Maintenance ship. I will go to Kenya and learn to read and write, and when I am ready, I will study to become an historian. And when I am a good enough historian, I will return to Kirinyaga and teach what I have learned."

"I am powerless to stop you from leaving," I said, "for the right to emigrate is guaranteed to all our citizens by our charter. But if you return, know that despite what we have been to one another, I will oppose you."

"I do not wish to be your enemy, Koriba," he said.

"I do not wish to have you as an enemy," I replied. "The bond between us has been a strong one."

"But the things I have learned are too important to my people."

"They are *my* people too," I pointed out, "and I have led them to this point by always doing what I think is best for them."

"Perhaps it is time for *them* to choose what is best."

"They are incapable of making that choice," I said.

"If they are incapable of making that choice, it is only because you have hoarded knowledge to which they have as much right as you do."

"Think very carefully before you do this thing," I said. "Despite my love for you, if you do anything to harm Kirinyaga, I will crush you like an insect."

He smiled sadly. "For six years I have asked you to teach me how to turn my enemies into insects so that I may crush them. Is this how I am finally to learn?"

I could not help but return his smile. I had an urge to stand up and throw my arms around him and hug him, but such behavior is unacceptable in a *mundumugu*, so I merely looked at him for a long moment and then said, "*Kwaheri*, Ndemi. You were the best of them."

"I had the best teacher," he replied.

And with that, he turned and began the long walk toward Haven.

The problems caused by Ndemi did not end with his departure.

Njoro dug a borehole near his hut, and when I explained that the Kikuyu did not dig boreholes but carried their water from the river, he replied that surely *this* borehole must be acceptable, for the idea came not from the Europeans but rather the Tswana people far to the south of Kenya.

I ordered the boreholes to be filled in. When Koinnage argued that there were crocodiles in the river and that he would not risk the lives of our women simply to maintain what he felt was a useless tradition, I had to threaten him with a powerful *thahu*, or curse—that of impotency—before he agreed.

Then there was Kidogo, who had named his firstborn Jomo, after Jomo Kenyatta, the Burning Spear. One day he announced that the boy was henceforth to be known as Johnstone, and I had to threaten him with banishment to another village before he relented. But even as he gave in,

Mbura changed his own name to Johnstone and moved to a distant village even before I could order it.

Shima continued to tell anyone who would listen that I had forced Ndemi to leave Kirinyaga because he was occasionally late for his lessons, and Koinnage kept requesting a computer that was the equal of my own.

Finally, young Mdutu created his own version of a barbed-wire enclosure for his father's cattle, using woven grasses and thorns, making sure he wrapped them around the fenceposts. I had it torn down, and thereafter he always walked away when the other children circled around me to hear a story.

I began to feel like the Dutch boy in Hans Christian Anderson's fairy tale. As quickly as I put my finger in the dike to staunch the flow of European ideas, they would break through in another place.

And then a strange thing happened. Certain ideas that were *not* European, that Ndemi could not possibly have transmitted to the members of the village, began cropping up on their own.

Kibo, the youngest of Koinnage's three wives, rendered the fat from a dead warthog and began burning it at night, creating Kirinyaga's first lamp. Ngobe, whose arm was not strong enough to throw a spear with any accuracy, devised a very primitive bow and arrow, the first Kikuyu ever to use such a weapon. Karenja created a wooden plow, so that his ox could drag it through the fields while he wives simply guided it, and soon all the other villagers were improvising plows and strangely-shaped digging tools. Indeed, alien ideas that had been dormant since the creation of Kirinyaga were now springing forth on all fronts. Ndemi's words had opened a Pandora's box, and I did not know how to close it.

I spent many long days sitting alone on my hill, staring down at the village and wondering if a Utopia can evolve and still remain a Utopia.

And the answer was always the same: Yes, but it will not be the *same* Utopia, and it was my sacred duty to keep Kirinyaga a Kikuyu Utopia.

When I was convinced that Ndemi was not going to return, I began going down to the village each day, trying to decide which of the children was the brightest and most forceful, for it would take both brilliance and force to deflect the alien ideas which were infecting our world and turning it into something it was never meant to be.

I spoke only to the boys, for no female may be a *mundumugu*. Some, like Mdutu, had already been corrupted by listening to Ndemi —but those who had *not* been corrupted by Ndemi were even more hopeless, for a mind cannot open and close at will, and those who were unmoved by what he had to say were not bright enough for the tasks a *mundumugu* must perform.

I expanded my search to other villages, convinced that somewhere on Kirinyaga I would find the boy I sought, a boy who grasped the difference between facts, which merely informed, and parables, which not only informed but *instructed.* I needed a Homer, a Jesus, a Shakespeare, someone who could touch men's souls and gently guide them down the path that must be taken.

But the more I searched, the more I came to the realization that a Utopia does not lend itself to such tellers of tales. Kirinyaga seemed divided into two totally separate groups: those who were content with their lives and had no need to think, and those whose every thought led them farther and farther from the society we had labored to build. The unimaginative would never be capable of creating parables, and the imaginative would create their own parables, parables that would not reaffirm a belief in Kirinyaga and a distrust of alien ideas.

After some months I was finally forced to concede that, for whatever reason, there were no potential *mundumugus* waiting to be found and groomed. I began wondering if Ndemi had been truly unique, or if he would have eventually rejected my teachings even without exposure to the European influence of the computer. Was it possible that a true Utopia could not outlast the generation that founded it, that it was the nature of man to reject the values of the society into which he is born, even when those values are sacred?

Or was it just conceivable that Kirinyaga had *never* been a Utopia, that somehow we had deluded ourselves into believing that we could go back to a way of life that had forever vanished?

I considered that possibility for a long time, but eventually I rejected it, for if it were true, then the only logical conclusion was that it had vanished because the Europeans' values were more pleasing to Ngai than our own, and this I knew to be false.

No, if there was a truth anywhere in the universe, it was that Kirinyaga was exactly as it was meant to be—and if Ngai felt obligated to test us by presenting us with these heresies, that would make our ultimate victory over the lies of the Europeans all the more sweet. If minds were worth anything, they were worth fighting for, and when Ndemi returned, armed with his facts and his data and his numbers, he would find me waiting for him.

It would be a lonely battle, I thought as I carried my empty water gourds down to the river, but having given His people a second chance to build their Utopia, Ngai would not allow us to fail. Let Ndemi tempt our people with his history and his passionless statistics. Ngai had His own weapon, the oldest and truest weapon He possessed, the weapon that had created Kirinyaga and kept it pure and intact despite all the many challenges it had encountered.

I looked into the water and studied the weapon critically. It appeared old and frail, but I could also see hidden reservoirs of strength, for although the future appeared bleak, it could not fail as long as it was used in Ngai's service. It stared back at me, bold and unblinking, secure in the rightness of its cause.

It was the face of Koriba, last storyteller among the Kikuyu, who stood ready to battle once again for the soul of his people.

## Introduction to "Inquiry into the Auction of the United States of America"

This was written for one of the hardcover Pulphouse magazines (back in the earlies, as Trader Horn might say).

The idea was simple enough: Ronald Reagan has just quadrupled the national debt, the stock market wasn't doing much of anything that year, and OPEC still knew how to use its power.

This was the likely, if sardonic, result.

# INQUIRY INTO THE AUCTION OF THE UNITED STATES OF AMERICA

On October 11, 2016, the United States of America, including all of its assets, was offered at public auction.

***

*Statement from Secretary of the Treasury William P. Compton:* "It's just simple mathematics. Our national debt now stands at something over 13 trillion dollars, and our annual revenues are insufficient to pay off the interest, let alone the principal. When there is no practical means of meeting one's basic expenses, then liquidation of assets is the only viable solution."

***

*Statement from Shiekh Ali ben Hariff of Saudi Arabia:* "Unquestionably it was a failure to adjust. For example, when Kinosaka of Japan made his breakthrough and gave the world an inexpensive way to convert to solar power, we Arabs didn't swim upstream against the tide of events. We didn't bare our fighting fangs against the Dentist of Destiny. No, we covered up our oil fields with public parks and quaint little brokerage houses of gossamer gaiety. Of course, owning a third of the world's banking houses *did* make the transition easier..."

***

*Statement from Hubert Jameson, Chairman of the Board of the now-defunct Standard Oil Company:* "What the hell were we supposed to do—throw five million people out of work because some little Chink or Jap or whatever the hell he was found a way to bottle the Sun? Sure we fought to stay in business! After all, fossil fuels won us the first two World Wars, didn't they? Abe Lincoln lit his lamps with oil, didn't he? George Washington...well, forget about George Washington. Anyway, it would have been unpatriotic to give up without a fight."

***

*Statement from Richard J. Daley IV, Chairman of the Chicago Transit Authority (C.T.A.):* "Yes, I realize that our fares have increased eight thousand percent in the past decade, and no, the C.T.A. is not dependant upon fossil fuels to any great extent. What we really have here is a situation in which, thanks to soaring gas prices, a finite number of trains and buses was being asked to transport an almost infinite number of commuters. The logistics of the problem, and the expenditures in time and manpower, became so great that we decided the only way to handle so much business was, paradoxically, to drive it away. Hence, every time there was a price increase in fossil fuels, we matched it penny for penny. This policy has worked out so well that only last week we laid off half our drivers, engineers, and conductors, and put the rest on part-time. Thus, once again, modern management has met the challenge."

***

*Statement from Edwin Kominski, Comptroller of the United States of America:* "Of course, there are a lot of details to be worked out yet. Will Lockheed still owe seventy billion dollars to the new government? Who will pay off our national debt? Can the Los Angeles Raiders still move to Butte, Montana? Will a general tax amnesty be declared? It's a tricky situation."

***

*Statement from Clarissa Wyatt, Estate Appraiser for Southby's:* "My own feeling is that they'd be better off selling the national parks, the Great Lakes, and the Las Vegas hotels separately. Put everything into one big package that includes such undesireable locations as Manhattan and Los Angeles, and the price has got to decrease accordingly. A guess? Oh, I would estimate that it should bring at least 35 billion. I mean, the buildings alone have to be worth that much. Of course, they'll all have to be converted to solar power—but even so, 30 billion would be the rock-bottom minimum. Maybe 28."

***

*Statement from Harvey Purple Cloud, Hereditary Chief of the Mescalaro Apaches:* "Make a bid? Like, man, you gotta be pulling my leg! We gave those turkeys a perfectly nice little piece of real estate, and look what they did to it."

***

*Statement from Big Frank Stephens, President of the Brotherhood of Coal Miners' Local #403:* "They try to convert without using my union and I'll pull out every miner from here to Albany, and then let's see how warm they keep this winter while they're putting in half a trillion solar batteries!"

***

*Statement from Eugene V. Hagermann, Professor of History at Yale University:* "No, I definitely wouldn't liken this to the fall of the Roman Empire. For one thing, Christianity and military overexpansion have nothing to do with our current situation. For another, the Romans had class."

★★★

*Statement from Frederick J. Allenby, Chairman of the Board of Exxon Power Company:* "Look, a corporation that can't keep up with the times is bound to go under. We're sorry about Standard and Shell and Mobil, but that's the way the cookie crumbles. I'd like to go into the subject in more detail, but I'm a little pressed for time right now. I'm getting together with some astronomers up at Mt. Palomar to determine a proper solar depletion allowance."

★★★

On October 14, 2016, the United States of America was sold to the Republic of Yemen for 22.4 billion dollars. The underbidder was the still-unsettled estate of Howard Hughes.

Payment was made in Japanese yen.

## Introduction to "Costigan's Wager"

This is probably the strangest story I've written. When the Orlando Worldcon committee was bidding to host the 1992 convention (which they won), they were looking for ways to raise money. One of the more popular methods was to have eight well-known writers each write a story of less than 250 words, which would be printed on a bookmark, the flip side of which advertised the Orlando bid. Believe it or not, complete sets bring a tidy price at auction these days.

I determined not to do a pun—that struck me as a cop-out. Well, let me tell you—you'd be surprised how hard it is to tell a story with a legitimate plot in less than 250 words.

# COSTIGAN'S WAGER

"Your move," said Satan.

"Don't rush me," muttered Costigan irritably as he surveyed the board.

"It's not as if we're playing for something important, like political power," said Satan. "The stakes are really quite trivial."

"There's nothing trivial about my soul."

"Have you ever seen it?" scoffed Satan. "Do you ever use it? Of course not. If I win, you'll never miss it."

"And if I win, I'll be up to my neck in money and beautiful women," replied Costigan. "So shut up and let me concentrate."

Satan fell silent, and after another moment of thoughtful consideration, Costigan moved his unprotected queen to King's Bishop Five. Satan pounced on the sacrifice, never noticed the two rooks lurking in the background, found himself immediately on the defensive, and resigned after the 29th move of the game.

★ ★ ★

"What's going on?" demanded Costigan as he surveyed his infernal surroundings.

"Welcome to hell, Mr. Costigan," said Satan with a truly Satanic grin.

"We had a bet! I won!"

"So you did, Mr. Costigan, so you did."

"Then what am I doing here?"

"Didn't anyone ever tell you," said Satan, just before he threw his latest victim into the fiery pits, "that gambling is a sin? And we all know what happens to sinners, don't we?"

His amused laughter filled what was left of Costigan's universe.

## Introduction to "My Girl"

One morning Marion Zimmer Bradley called me out of the blue and asked if I'd contribute something to her *Marion Zimmer Bradley's Fantasy Magazine.*

I said sure. Then I sat down and tried to come up with a fantasy idea for her.

They were re-running *Dracula* that night on AMC or Turner Classics. It was all the impetus I needed.

# MY GIRL

Dear Sid:

Sorry I haven't written for awhile, but a lot has been happening in my life lately. For one thing, I've changed jobs a couple of times. (Well, to be honest, I was *ordered* to change jobs. By my ex-bosses. Seems I keep oversleeping, which is something I never used to do. Let me tell you, buddy, middle age is a bitch.)

As you can see from the return address, I've moved into a new place. No pool or exercise room at this complex, but lately I've been too dragged out to swim or do the weights anyway, and the rent is half what I used to pay. The crazy thing is that in spite of leading a more sedentary life, I've managed to lose close to 30 pounds. You'd hardly recognize me these days.

Still, it's not all bad news. I've got a new girl. And *what* a girl! No more playing the field for *this* boy. I've found everything I ever wanted in one delicious French morsel. (Or maybe she's Belgian. Or Czech. Or even Russian. Who cares? All I know is that she's got an accent, and French sounds sexier, you know what I mean?)

Let me tell you about her, because she's changed my whole life. Her name is Michelle, and she's got the softest, whitest skin you've ever seen. We've got a lot in common, Michelle and me. I've always been a party animal, but I can't hold a candle to her. She seems to come alive at night, and she can keep going until five or six every morning.

(Remember Janni, the last girl I wrote you about? I thought we really had something there, but it turned out that she was an [ugh!] Morning Person. That's probably why it didn't last. Total incompatability.)

For all that she loves nightlife, Michelle's strangely unsophisticated in ways, too. Like the first time I took her out to dinner: I'd been boning up so I could imnpress her with my knowledge of the wine list, and just as I'm deciding between a cabernet and a chardonnay, she tells me she doesn't drink...wine. (A European who doesn't drink wine? Who the hell ever heard of such a thing?)

So I offer to buy her a whiskey, or a Scotch, or even a beer, and it turns out she doesn't drink *anything*. I can't believe it, so I run down the list until I come to a Bloody Mary, and suddenly her eyes light up and she agrees to try one—but when it arrives she just looks at it, mutters something about tomato juice, and shoves it aside. (Well, at least she's not a lush like Judy. Remember Judy? The one who threw up all over the back seat of your Lincoln? By the way, did I ever send you a check to cover getting it shampooed?)

Anyway, this isn't to say that Michelle's not a lot of fun, or that she needs alcohol to overcome her inhibitions. In point of fact, she hasn't *got* any. Inhibitions, I mean. My back is *covered* with scratches, and while I don't remember much about our romantic interludes—*I* still drink, even if she doesn't— let me tell you that this girl gives one dynamite hickey. I finally bought an Ascot to cover it, so I don't have to keep answering embarrassing questions at the office.

Still, when she needs to, she can also come up with those exquisite European manners. I took her over to Dick's house Tuesday night, and we visited Pat and Roger last weekend, and she refused to enter either place until they invited her in. I kind of like that. I'm sure the others wrote it off as shyness, but as I see it she was forcing the people around her to be just as well-mannered as she is—kind of like the way a good point guard makes all his teammates better.

By the way, have I mentioned yet that she's drop-dead gorgeous? Well, she is. You'd figure a girl who looks half as good as Michelle would have mirrors everywhere. I mean, hell, if I looked like Mel Gibson or Robert Redford, you can bet *I'd* never be far from one. But no one can say my Michelle is your typically vain female. Believe it or not, she hasn't got a mirror in her whole house. Not even in the bathroom. Now, is that old-fashioned modesty, or what?

Of course, nobody looks that good by accident, and she's really into watching her weight—and since we're spending so much time together, I seem to be watching mine as well. That might be my only regret about the whole thing: no more Italian food. Every time I offer to take her down to Tony's for a pizza or some veal scallopini, she makes a face and tells me that the smell of garlic makes her sick.

Still, it's not a total loss. Believe it or not, I'm actually broadening my gastronomic horizons. Yeah, old conservative me. Michelle's put me onto some exotic European dishes: chocolate-covered ants and fried grasshoppers. (One night I teased her that all she eats are bugs. You know what she answered? "Worms are nice, too." Said it with a perfectly straight face, too. How many girls have a sense of humor like that?)

Finally, there's an aura of Mystery about her, just like all those heroines in the 1940's B movies. I can't quite put my finger on it, but I have a feeling there's a tragedy somewhere in her past, and I think it has to do with someone she loved getting drowned. At any rate, while she'll join or meet me in some of the grubbiest areas of town, I can't get her to walk on any of the bridges that cross the river. It's like someone she knew must have fallen in once, and now she's got this subconscious fear of ever being over a body of water.

And I guess when you lose someone you care for, it makes you more compassionate toward the whole world in general. You want a crazy example? One night I hear bats flapping around in the eaves of her house, and I offer to call Joey Goldberg. (You remember little Joey, who used to be the water boy for the football team back in high school? Well, he's got his own company now. Exterminates every kind of pest short of I.R.S. auditors.) Anyway, she tells me bats have a right to live, too, and if I ever suggest killing one again, we're quits. How's that for a caring, 90's kind of girl? I mean, hell, she's so sensitive that we walk blocks out of our way just so we don't have to pass the Catholic cemetery over on Elm Street. I guess the sight of all those graves and crosses must depress her.

Well, I should probably close now and head off to bed. I'm getting a little pale—too much time in the office, I suppose— so I'm hitting the tanning parlor every morning before I go to work. Hasn't done much good yet, but I suppose these things take time.

Your pal,
Harvey

PS: Just out of curiosity, do you know if the FDA or anyone like that has ever looked into the tanning parlor business? There's probably no connection, but ever since I started going I seem to be so short of energy that I'm just dragging all the time.

PPS: Michelle called since I finished writing the last sentence. Says she's thirsty and wants to come over. Can you believe it? Three in the morning, and she's coming to my apartment for a drink. What a girl!

## Introduction to "Darker Than You Wrote"

When Roger Zelazny phoned me and asked me to contribute to a "tribute anthology" to be called *The Williamson Effect*, I agreed instantly. Jack Williamson has been my friend for a third of a century, and I thought this would be a way to repay some of his many kindnesses.

My favorite of Jack's books has always been his classic fantasy, *Darker Than You Think*, so I decided to use that as a jumping-off point.

If nothing else, the story proves beyond any doubt that Jack is a man of exquisite taste.

# DARKER THAN YOU WROTE

You lied, Jack.

Yeah, I know, you had to change his name to Will Barbee for legal reasons. I have no problem with that. And you embellished a little here and a little there. That's okay; it's what novelists do.

But you know what they say about Karen Blixen's *Out of Africa*—that every single sentence is true, but the book, taken as a whole, is a lie?

Same thing with *Darker Than You Think*.

You took Jacob Bratzinger—I'm sorry: Will Barbee; whoever heard of a protagonist called Bratzinger?—and romanticized the hell out of him. Made him some kind of hero. Even gave him a happy ending. You did all that just to make a sale.

Well, let me state just for the record that he wasn't romantic, and he was no hero, and, above all, he didn't end happily.

I know. I was there.

I'm sure shrinks hear a lot of strange stories during their working hours. So do fantasy editors and Hollywood producers, and any tourist who ever tries to walk past a beggar in a Third World city. But let me tell you, *nobody* hears as much out-and-out unbelievable bullshit as your friendly neighborhood bartender.

That's me.

I remember that Jake used to come around in the afternoons. A lonely drinker. Never had anyone with him, never tried to make friends with anyone once he got here. Stayed down at the far end of the bar and minded his own business. Always had an expression on his face that made you hope he was drinking to forget and that he'd succeed, because it looked like what he was remembering was pretty grim stuff.

He always left before sundown. Made no difference to me: I figured he worked a night shift. But then he started coming in all torn up, like he spent his nights prizefighting. Except that he wasn't black-and-blue, the way you'd expect him to be after a fight. No, sir, he was all ripped up, just like I said. He healed pretty fast, didn't bother going to the doctor except for some of the more serious wounds, never complained about the pain.

Since he usually showed up around two or maybe two-thirty, and he left before six, he and I spent a lot of time together with nobody else around, and finally, after maybe half a year, he loosened up and started telling me his story. I didn't believe it at first, but what the hell, it helped pass the time, so I dummied up and listened to him.

I gather that he was telling it to you at pretty much the same time, maybe in the mornings, and he kept waiting for your book to come out. He was sure some scientist would read about him and do something to cure him, though in retrospect I don't know what they could have done.

But then you crossed him up, Jack. You changed his name and gave him a girlfriend and passed it off as science fiction. You'll never know how close he came to killing you when *Darker Than You Think* came out.

Only one thing stopped him, and that was that he was sick of killing. You know, if he'd been a werewolf, if lycanthropy was all there was to it, if the old legends were right, I think he could have adjusted, I really do.

But you know that wasn't true, and you even told your readers. Jake didn't turn into a wolf. Not him. He was a tiger one day, and a roc—you called him a pterosaur—the next. He knew a girl—he wasn't involved with her, he just happened to share a hunting ground—named June (you called her April, remember?) who became a she-wolf at nights. And then there was Ben Sacks—you wrote him out of the book completely—who was a puma.

And even knowing all that, knowing that the flesh-eaters weren't confined to one kind of body, that they weren't all wolves or vampire bats or any of the other creatures out of legend, you still didn't see it, you never drew the connection.

But Jake learned it early on, and so did all of the others. He didn't shrivel in the sunlight like some bad Dracula movie, you know. He didn't instantly turn back into a man, either. It was a slow process, a gradual transformation, that took maybe ten or twelve minutes.

And during that time, he learned the awful, hideous truth, not about himself but about his world. Our world. For just as followers outnumber leaders and prey outnumber predators, so did those humans who turned into sheep and goats and cattle far outnumber Jake and his kind. It was presumptuous of him—and you —to think that only a handful of men and women underwent the Change at nights, or that those who changed all became nocturnal hunters.

Jake would make his kills, clean and swift, in the dead of night. He'd drag the carcasses to places of safety, where competing carnivores couldn't see or scent them. And then he'd dine on them, as he was meant to dine: tearing at their flesh, lapping up their blood, swallowing huge mouthfuls of meat. It was perfectly natural.

Until morning came, and the Change began, and it afflicted both predator and prey, and he'd find himself crouching over a half-eaten child, or a partially-consumed woman, and he realized how true was the old saying that you are what you eat, and he was once again a man.

He hated himself for it. His only hope was your book, and then you turned it into a novel, and after that he didn't have any hope at all. He started drinking more heavily, and the haunted look in his eyes grew worse and worse.

It only took another two weeks before he put a gun to his head, right there in the bar, and blew his brains out. Yeah, I know you hadn't heard, Jack; he asked me not to tell you.

That was, let me see, damned near half a century ago. Of course, I don't age the way normal men do. No reason why I should; I'm no more normal than Jake was. The Change just hit me a little later, that's all.

His very last wish was that I avenge him. It took me a long time to figure out what he meant. I mean, hell, he killed himself, so I could hardly take my vengeance out on him. And while it's true that the world made him what he was, I wouldn't begin to know how to destroy the world. So I thought about it, and thought about it, and finally I decided that he meant I should pay you a visit, Jack. He counted on that book of yours, and you let him down. I finally sold my business and retired last month, so now I'm ready to do what has to be done.

They tell me you're a pretty smart fellow, and that you're still working well into your eighties. That's good; I admire brains and industry. I figure you're probably a racoon, or maybe a badger.

Me, I'm a wolverine. And unlike Jake Bratzinger, I don't have a problem with guilt at all. I *like* meat.

See you soon, Jack.

## Introduction to "The Roosevelt Dispatches"

It was in the airport on the way home from Conadian, the 1994 Worldcon held in Winnipeg, that Kevin Anderson walked up and asked me to contribute to *War of the Worlds: Global Dispatches*, an anthology he had just sold.

The premise was this: we were to (fictionally) accept H. G. Wells' Martian invasion as true, and have various historical characters react to it.

I chose Teddy Roosevelt, of course. (Over the years he has become my personal property in terms of alternate history stories; this was his sixth go-round in a Resnick story.)

It was difficult to write, since our characters were faced with a world-threatening problem, and we were not permitted to let them solve it, since Wells himself solved it at the end of his book. So I took my cue from the title of the anthology and went from there.

# THE ROOSEVELT DISPATCHES

*Excerpt from the Diary of Theodore Roosevelt (Volume 23):*

*July 9, 1898:* Shot and killed a most unusual beast this afternoon. Letters of inquiry go off tomorrow to the various museums to see which of them would like the mounted specimen once I have finished studying it.

Tropical rain continues unabated. Many of the men are down with influenza, and in the case of poor Westmore it looks like we shall lose him to pneumonia before the week is out.

Still awaiting orders, now that San Juan Hill and the surrounding countryside are secured. It may well be that we should remain here until we know that the island is totally free from any more of the creatures that I shot this afternoon.

It's quite late. Just time for a two-mile run and a chapter of Jane Austen, and then off to bed.

★ ★ ★

*Letter from Theodore Roosevelt to F. C. Selous, July 12, 1898:*

My Dear Selous:

I had the most remarkable experience in Cuba this week, one that I feel compelled to share with you.

I had just led my Rough Riders in a victorious campaign in Cuba. We were still stationed there, awaiting orders to return home. With nothing better to do, I spent many happy hours bird-watching, and the event in question occurred late one afternoon when I was making my way through a riverine forest in search of the Long-billed Curlew.

Afternoon had just passed into twilight, and as I made my way through the dense vegetation I had the distinct feeling that I was no longer alone, that an entity at least as large as myself was lurking nearby. I couldn't imagine what it might be, for to the best of my knowledge the tapir and the jaguar do not inhabit the islands of the Caribbean.

I proceeded more cautiously, and in another twenty yards I came to a halt and found myself facing a *thing* the size of one of our American grizzlies. The only comparably-sized animal within your experience would probably be the mountain gorilla, but this creature was at least thirty percent larger than the largest of the silverbacks.

The head was round, and was totally without a nose! The eyes were large, dark, and quite widely spread. The mouth was V-shaped and lipless, and drooled constantly.

It was brown—not the brown of an impala or a koodoo, but rather the slick moist brown of a sea-slug, its body glistening as if greased. The thing had no arms as such, but it did have a number of long, sinewy tentacles, each seemingly the thickness and strength of an elephant's trunk.

It took one look at me, made a sound that was half-growl and half-roar, and charged. I had no idea of its offensive capabilities, but I didn't like the look of those tentacles, so I quickly raised my Winchester to my shoulder and fired at almost point-blank range. I could hear the *smack!* of the bullet as it bounced off the trunk of the beast's body. The creature continued to approach me, and I hurled myself aside at the last instant, barely avoiding two of its outstretched tentacles.

I rolled as I hit the ground, and fired once more from a prone position, right into the open V of its mouth. This time there was a reaction, and a violent one. The thing hooted noisily and began tearing up pieces of the turf, all the while shaking its head vigorously. Within seconds it was literally uprooting large bushes and shredding them as if they were no more than mere tissue paper.

I waited until it was facing in my direction again and put a bullet into its left eye. Again, the reaction was startling: the creature began ripping apart nearby trees and screaming at such a pitch that all the nearby bird life fled in terror.

By that point I must confess that I was looking for some means of retreat, for I know of no animal that could take a rifle bullet in the mouth and another in the eye and still remain not just standing but aggressive and formidable. I trained my rifle on the brute and began backing away.

My movement seemed to have caught its attention, for suddenly it ceased its ravings and turned to face me. Then it began advancing slowly and purposefully—and a moment later it did something that no animal anywhere in the world has ever done: it produced a weapon.

The thing looked like a sword, but when the creature pointed it at me, a beam of light shot out of it, missing me only by inches, and instantly setting the bush beside me ablaze. I jumped in the opposite direction as it fired its sword of heat again, and again the forest combusted in a blinding conflagration.

I turned and raced back the way I had come. After perhaps sixty yards I chanced a look back, and saw that the creature was following me. However, despite its many physical attributes, speed was not to be counted among them. I used that to my advantage, putting enough distance between us so that it lost sight of me. I then jumped into the nearby river, making sure that no water should invade my rifle. Here, at least, I felt safe from the indirect effects of the creature's heat weapon.

It came down the path some forty seconds later. Rather than shooting it immediately, I let it walk by while I studied it, looking for vulnerable areas. The thing bore no body armour as such, not even the type of body plating that our mutual friend Corbett describes on the Indian rhino, yet its skin seemed impervious to bullets. Its body, which I now could see in its entirety, was almost perfectly spherical except for the head and tentacles, and there were no discernable weak or thin spots where head and tentacles joined the trunk.

Still, I couldn't let it continue along the path, because sooner or later it would come upon my men, who were totally unprepared for it. I looked for an earhole, could not find one, and with only the back of its head to shoot at felt that I could not do it any damage. So I stood up, waist deep in the water, and yelled at it. It turned toward me, and as it did so I put two more bullets into its left eye.

Its reaction was the same as before, but much shorter in duration. Then it regained control of itself, stared balefully at me through both eyes—the good one and the one that had taken three bullets—and began walking toward me, weapon in hand... and therein I thought I saw a way in which I might finally disable it.

I began walking backward in the water, and evidently the creature felt some doubt about its weapon's accuracy, because it entered the water and came after me. I stood motionless, my sights trained on the sword of heat. When the creature was perhaps thirty yards from me, it came to a halt and raised its weapon—and as it did so, I fired.

The sword of heat flew from the creature's hand, spraying its deadly light in all directions. Then it fell into the water, its muzzle—if that is the right word, and I very much suspect that it isn't—pointing at the creature. The water around it began boiling and hissing as steam rose, and the creature screeched once and sank beneath the surface of the river.

It took about five minutes before I felt safe in approaching it—after all, I had no idea how long it could hold its breath —but sure enough, as I had hoped, the beast was dead.

I have never before seen anything like it, and I will be stuffing and mounting this specimen for either the American Museum or the Smithsonian. I'll send you a copy of my notes, and hopefully a number of photographs taken at various stages of the post mortem examination and the mounting.

I realize that I was incredibly lucky to have survived. I don't know how many more such creatures exist here in the jungles of Cuba, but they are too malevolent to be allowed to survive and wreak their havoc on the innocent locals here. They must be eradicated, and I know of no hunter with whom I would rather share this expedition than yourself. I will put my gun and my men at your disposal, and hopefully we can rid the island of this most unlikely and lethal aberration.

Yours,

Roosevelt

★ ★ ★

*Letter to Carl Akeley, hunter and taxidermist, c/o The American Museum of Natural History, July 13, 1898:*

Dear Carl:

Sorry to have missed you at the last annual banquet, but as you know, I've been preoccupied with matters here in Cuba.

Allow me to ask you a purely hypothetical question: could a life form exist that has no stomach or digestive tract? Let me further hypothesize that this life form ingests the blood of its prey—other living creatures—directly into its veins.

First, is it possible?

Second, could such a form of nourishment supply sufficient energy to power a body the size of, say, a grizzly bear?

I realize that you are a busy man, but while I cannot go into detail, I beg you to give these questions your most urgent attention.

Yours very truly,

Theodore Roosevelt

★ ★ ★

*Letter to Dr. Charles Doolittle Walcott, Secretary of the Smithsonian Institution, July 13, 1898:*

Dear Charles:

I have a strange but, please believe me, very serious question for you.

Can a complex animal life form exist without gender? Could it possibly reproduce—don't laugh—by budding? Could a complex life form reproduce by splitting apart, as some of our single-celled animals do?

Please give me your answers soonest.

Yours very truly,

Theodore Roosevelt

★ ★ ★

*Excerpts from monograph submitted by Theodore Roosevelt on July 14, 1898 for publication by the American Museum of Natural History:*

...The epidermis is especially unique, not only in its thickness and pliability, but also in that there is no layer of subcutaneous fat, nor can I discern any likely source for the secretion of the oily liquid that covers the entire body surface of the creature.

One of the more unusual features is the total absence of a stomach, intestine, or any other internal organ that could be used for digestion. My own conclusion, which I hasten to add is not based on observation, is that nourishment is ingested directly into the bloodstream from the blood of other animals.

The V-shaped mouth was most puzzling, for what use can a mouth be to a life form that has no need of eating? But as I continued examining the creature, I concluded that I was guilty of a false assumption, based on the placement of the "mouth". The V-shaped opening is not a mouth at all, but rather a breathing orifice, which I shall not call a nose simply because it is also the source of the creature's vocalizations, if I may so term the growls and shrieks that emanate from it...

Perhaps the most interesting feature of the eye is not the multi-faceted pupil, nor even the purple-and-brown cornea, which doubtless distorts its ability to see colors as we do, but rather the bird-like nictitating membrane, (or haw, as this inner eyelid is called in dogs) which protects it from harm. Notice that although it could not possibly have known the purpose or effects of my rifle, it nonetheless managed to lower it quickly enough to shield the eye from the main force of my bullet. Indeed, as is apparent from even a cursory examination of the haw, the healing process is so incredibly rapid that although I shot it three times in the left eye, the three wounds are barely discernable, even though the bullets passed entirely through the haw and buried themselves at the back of the eye.

I cannot believe that the creature's color can possibly be considered protective coloration...but then, I do not accept the concept of protective coloration to begin with. Consider the zebra: were it brown or black, it would be no easier to spot at, say, a quarter mile, than a wildebeest or topi or prong-horned deer—but because God saw fit to give it black and white stripes, it stands out at more than half a mile, giving notice of its presence to all predators, thereby negating the notion of protective coloration, for the zebra's stripes are, if anything, anti-protective, and yet it is one of the most successful animals in Africa. Thus, while the creature I shot is indeed difficult to pick out in what I assume to be its natural forest surroundings, I feel that it is brown by chance rather than design.

...Field conditions are rather primitive here, but I counted more than one hundred separate muscles in the largest of the tentacles, and must assume there are at least another two hundred that I was unable to discern. This is the only section of the body that seems criss-crossed with nerves, and it is conceivable that if the creature can be slowed by shock, a bullet placed in the cluster of nerves and blood vessels where the tentacle joins the trunk of the body will do the trick...

The brain was a surprise to me. It is actually three to four times larger and heavier, in proportion to the body, than a man's brain is in proportion to his body. This, plus the fact that the creature used a weapon (which, alas, was lost in the current of the river), leads me to the startling but inescapable conclusion that what we have here is a species of intelligence at least equal to, and probably greater than, our own.

Respectfully submitted on this 14th day of July, 1898, by

Theodore Roosevelt, Colonel

United States Armed Forces

* * *

*Letter to Willis Maynard Crenshaw, of Winchester Rifles, July 14, 1898:*

Dear Mr. Crenshaw:

Enclosed you will find a sample of skin from a newly-discovered animal. The texture is such that it is much thicker than elephant or rhinoceros hide, though it in no way resembles the skin of either pachyderm.

However, I'm not asking you to analyze the skin, at least not scientifically. What I want you to do is come up with a rifle and a bullet that will penetrate the skin.

Just as importantly, I shall need stopping power. Assume the animal will weigh just under a ton, but has remarkable vitality. Given the terrain, I'll most likely be shooting from no more than twenty yards, so I probably won't have time for too many second shots. The first shot *must* bring it down from the force of the bullet, even if no vital organs are hit.

Please let me know when you have a prototype that I can test in the field, and please make no mention of this to anyone except the artisans who will be working on the project.

Thank you.

Yours very truly,

Theodore Roosevelt

★ ★ ★

*Private hand-delivered message from Theodore Roosevelt to President William McKinley, July 17, 1898:*

Dear Mr. President:

Certain facts have come to my attention that makes it imperative that you neither recall the Rough Riders from the Island of Cuba, nor disband them upon signing the Armistice with Spain.

There is something here, on this island, that is so evil, so powerful, so inimical to all men, that I do not believe I am exaggerating when I tell you that the entire human race is threatened by its very existence. I will make no attempt to describe it, for should said description fall into the wrong hands we could start a national panic if it is believed or become figures of public ridicule if it is not.

You will simply have to trust me that the threat is a very real one. Furthermore, I urge you not to recall *any* of our troops, for if my suspicions are correct we may need all of them and still more.

Col. Theodore Roosevelt

"The Rough Riders"

★ ★ ★

*Letter to Secretary of War Daniel S. Lamont, July 20, 1898:*

Dear Daniel:

McKinley is a fool! I warned him of perhaps the greatest threat yet to the people of America, and indeed to the world, and he has treated it as a joke.

Listen to me: it is essential that you cancel the recall order immediately and let my Rough Riders remain in Cuba. Furthermore, I want the entire army on standby notice, and if you're wise you'll transfer at least half of our forces to Florida, for that seems the likeliest spot for the invasion to begin.

I will be coming to Washington to speak to McKinley personally and try to convince him of the danger facing us. Anything you can do to pave the way will be appreciated.

Regards,

Roosevelt

★ ★ ★

*Speech delivered from the balcony above the Columbia Restaurant, Tampa, Florida, August 3, 1898:*

My fellow Americans:

It has lately come to your government's attention that there is a threat to the national security—indeed, to the security of the world—that currently lurks in the jungles of Cuba. I have seen it with my own eyes, and I assure you that no matter what you may hear in the days and weeks to come, the danger is real and cannot be underestimated.

Shortly after my Rough Riders took San Juan Hill, I encountered something in the nearby jungle so incredible that a description of it would only arouse your skepticism and your disbelief. It was a creature, quite probably intelligent, the like of which has never before been seen on this Earth. I am and always have been a vociferous Darwinian, but despite my knowledge of the biological sciences, I cannot begin to hazard a guess concerning how this creature evolved.

What I *can* tell you is that it has developed the ability to create weapons unlike any we have seen, and that it has no compunction about using them against human beings. It is an evil and malevolent life form, and it must be eradicated before it can turn its hatred loose against innocent Americans.

I was fortunate enough to kill the one I encountered in Cuba, but where there is one there will certainly be more. The United States government was originally dubious about the veracity of my claim, but I gather than recent information forwarded to the White House and the State Department from England, where more of these creatures have appeared, has finally convinced them that I was telling the truth.

Thus far none of the creatures has been discovered in the United States, but I say to you that it would be foolhardy to wait until they are found before coming up with an appropriate response. Americans have always been willing to make sacrifices and take up arms to defend their country, and this will be no exception. These creatures may have had their momentary successes against Cuban peasants and an unprepared Great Britain, but I tell you confidently they have no chance against an army of motivated Americans, driven by the indomitable American spirit and displaying the unshakeable courage of all true Americans.

To us as a people it has been granted to lay the foundations of our national life on a new continent. We are the heirs of the ages, and yet we have had to pay few of the penalties which in old countries are exacted by the bygone hand of a dead civilization. We have not been obliged to fight for our existence against any alien challenge—until now. I believe we are up to the challenge, and I am convinced that you believe so too.

I am leaving for Miami tomorrow, and from there I will be departing for Cuba two days later, to lead my men into battle against however many of these creatures exist in the dank rotting jungles of that tropical island. I urge every red-blooded able-bodied American among you to join me on this greatest of adventures.

★ ★ ★

*Letter to Kermit, Theodore Junior, Archie and Quentin Roosevelt, August 5, 1898:*

Dear Boys:

Tomorrow I embark on a great and exciting safari. I'm sure the details will be wired back to the newspapers on a daily basis, but I promise that when I return we'll sit around a campfire at Sagamore Hill and I'll tell you all the stories that the press never reported. Not only that, but I will bring back a trophy for each and every one of you.

School will be starting before I return. I expect each of you to go to class prepared for his lessons, and to apply your minds as vigorously as you apply your bodies to the games you play at home. Had I been slow of wit *or* of body I would not have survived my initial encounter with the creatures I shall be hunting in the coming days and weeks. Always remember that *balance* is the key in all things.

Love,

Father

★ ★ ★

*Letter (# 1,317) to Edith Carow Roosevelt, August 5, 1898:*

My Dearest Edith:

My ship leaves tomorrow morning, so it will perhaps be some weeks before I have the opportunity to write to you again.

Shortly I shall be off on the greatest hunt of my life. Give my love to the children. I wish the boys were just a little bit older, so that I could take them along on what promises to be the most exciting endeavor of my life.

I am still trying to rid myself of the cold I picked up when I plunged into that river in Cuba, but other than that I feel fit as a bull moose. It will take a lot more than a strange beast and a runny nose to bring a true American to his knees. The coming days should be just bully!

Your Theodore

## Introduction to "The Kemosabee"

When Piers Anthony and Richard Gilliam invited me to contribute to *Tales of the Great Turtle*, an anthology of science fiction and fantasy stories about American Indians, I was a little hesitant. After all, I was sure all the major Indian figures like Geronimo and Sitting Bull and Crazy Horse would be taken, and the only fictional Indian I could remember was Tonto.

Then, a few days later, while channel-flipping between sports events, I came to the scene in the movie, *Cat Ballou*, where Cat's father explains that the Indians are one of the twelve lost tribes of Israel.

I ran right to the computer and knocked out "The Kemosabee" in less than 90 minutes. You are welcome to disagree, but I think it's one of the two or three funniest short stories I've ever written.

# THE KEMOSABEE

So me and the Masked Man, we decide to hook up and bring evildoers to justice, which is a pretty full-time occupation considering just how many of these *momzers* there are wandering the West. Of course, I don't work on Saturdays, but this is never a problem, since he's usually sleeping off Friday night's binge and isn't ready to get back in the saddle until about half past Monday.

We get along pretty well, though we don't talk much to each other—my English is a little rusty, and his Yiddish is non-existent—but we share our food when times are tough, and we're always saving each other's life, just like it says in the dime novels.

Now, you'd think two guys who spend a whole year riding together wouldn't have any secrets from each other, but actually that's not the case. We respect each other's privacy, and it is almost twelve months to the day after we form a team that we find ourselves answering a call of Nature at the very same time, and I look over at him, and I am so surprised I could just *plotz*, you know what I mean?

It's then that I start calling him Kemosabee, and finally one day he asks me what it means, and I tell him that it means "uncircumcized goy", and he kind of frowns and tells me that he doesn't know what *either* word means, so I sit him down and explain that Indians are one of the lost Hebrew tribes, only we aren't as lost as we're supposed to be, because Custer and the rest of those *meshugginah* soldiers keeps finding us and blowing us to smithereens. And the Kemosabee, he asks if Hebrew is a suburb of Hebron, and right away I see we've got an enormous cultural gap to overcome.

But what the hell, we're pardners, and we're doing a pretty fair job of ridding the West of horse thieves and stage robbers and other varmints, so I say, "Look, Kemosabee, you're a *mensch* and I'm proud to ride with you, and if you wanna get drunk and *shtup* a bunch of *shikses* whenever we go into town, that's your business and who am I to tell you what to do? But Butch Cavendish and his gang are giving me enough *tsouris* this month, so if we stop off at any Indian villages, let's let this be our little secret, okay?"

And the Kemosabee, who is frankly a lot quicker with his guns than his brain, just kind of frowns and looks hazy and finally nods his head, though I'm sure he doesn't know what he's nodding about.

Well, we ride on for another day or two, and finally reach his secret silver mine, and he melts some of it down and shoves it into his shells, and like always I ride off and hunt up Reb Running Bear and have him say Kaddish over the bullets, and when I hunt up the Masked Man again I find he has had the *chutzpah* to take on the whole Cavendish gang single-handed, and since they know he never shoots to kill and they ain't got any such compunctions, they leave him lying there for dead with a couple of new *pupiks* in his belly.

So I make a sled and hook it to the back of his horse, which he calls Silver but which he really ought to call White, or at least White With The Ugly Brown Blotch On His Belly, and I hop up my pony, and pretty soon we're in front of Reb Running Bear's teepee, and he comes out and looks at the Masked Man lying there with his ten-gallon stetson for a long moment, and then he turns to me and says, "You know, that has got to be the ugliest *yarmulkah* I've ever seen."

"This is my pardner," I say. "Some goniffs drygulched him. You got to make him well."

Reb Running Bear frowns. "He doesn't look like one of the Chosen People to me. Where was he *bar mitzvahed*?"

"He wasn't," I say. "But he's one of the Good Guys. He and I are cleaning up the West."

"Six years in Hebrew school and you settle for being a janitor?" he says.

"Don't give me a hard time," I said. "We got bad guys to shoot and wrongs to right. Just save the Kemosabee's life."

"The Kemosabee?" he repeats. "Would I be very far off the track if I surmised that he doesn't keep kosher?"

"Look," I say, deciding that it's time to play hardball, "I hadn't wanted to bring this up, but I know what you and Mrs. Screaming Hawk were doing last time I visited this place."

"Keep your voice down or that *yenta* I married will make my life hell!" he whispers, glancing back toward his teepee. Then he grimaces. "Mrs. Screaming Hawk. Serves me right for taking her to Echo Canyon. *Feh!*"

I stare at him. "So *nu*?"

"All right, all right, Jehovah and I will nurse the Kemosabee back to health."

"Good," I say.

He glares at me. "But just this one time. Then I pass the word to all the other Rabbis: we don't cure no more *goys.* What have they ever done for us?"

Well, I am all prepared to argue the point, because I'm a pretty open-minded kind of guy, but just then the Kemosabee starts moaning and I realize that if I argue for more than a couple of minutes we could all be sitting *shivah* for him before dinnertime, so I wander off and pay a visit to Mrs. Rutting Elk to console her on the sudden passing of her husband and see if there is anything I can do to cheer her up, and Reb Running Bear gets to work, and lo and behold, in less than a week the Masked Man is up and around and getting impatient to go out after desperados, so we thank Reb Running Bear for his services, and he loads my pardner down with a few canteens of chicken soup, and we say a fond *shalom* to the village.

I am hoping we have a few weeks for the Kemosabee to regain his strength, of which I think he is still missing an awful lot, but as Fate would have it, we are riding for less than two hours when we come across the Cavendish gang's trail.

"Aha!" he says, studying the hoofprints. "All thirty of them! This is our chance for revenge!"

My first thought is to say something like, "What do you mean *we*, mackerel eater?"—but then I remember that Good Guys never back down from a challenge, so I simply say "Ugh!", which is my opinion of taking on thirty guys at once, but which he insists on interpreting as an affirmative.

We follow the trail all day, and when it's too dark to follow it any longer, we make camp on a small hill.

"We should catch up with them just after sunrise," says the Masked Man, and I can see that his trigger finger is getting itchy.

"Ugh," I say.

"We'll meet them on the open plain, where nobody can hide."

"Double ugh with cherries on it," I say.

"You look very grim, old friend," he says.

"Funny you should mention it," I say, but before I can suggest that we just forget the whole thing, he speaks again.

"You can have the other twenty-nine, but Cavendish is mine."

"You're all heart, Kemosabee," I say.

He stands up, stretches, and walks over to his bedroll. "Well, we've got a hard day's bloodletting ahead of us. We'd best get some sleep."

He lays down, and ten seconds later he's snoring like all get-out, and I sit there staring at him, and I just know he's not gonna come through this unscathed, and I remember Reb Running Bear's promise that no medicine man would ever again treat a goy.

And the more I think about it, the more I think that it's up to me, the loyal sidekick, to do something about it. And finally it occurs to me just what I have to do, because if I can't save him from the Cavendish gang, the least I can do is save him from himself.

So I go over to my bedroll, and pull out a bottle of Mogen David, and pour a little on my hunting knife, and try to remember the exact words the medicine man recites during the *bris*, and I know that someday, when he calms down, he'll thank me for this.

In the meantime, I'm gonna have to find a new nickname for for my pardner.

## Introduction to "Interview With the Almighty"

Kurt Roth cornered me on the Delphi network one night and asked for a funny story to lead off the first issue of a new prozine called *Quantum*.

It occurred to me that I hadn't given God any speaking parts lately—I used to turn out at least one story a year in which He has something to say—so I decided it was time to sit down face-to-face with Him and interview Him.

Here's the result.

# INTERVIEW WITH THE ALMIGHTY

RESNICK: I'm sitting here with God in Sid & Sylvia's 5-Star Deli. The tape recorder's on, and we're ready to go.

GOD: Relax. Have a knosh. They tell me the chopped liver is outstanding.

RESNICK: Can you tell me why you've agreed to this interview, after being silent for so long?

GOD: I hadn't realized that no one knew how to write the last time I gave one.

RESNICK: Can you tell us a little about your background?

GOD: Sure. In the beginning, I created the heavens and the earth.

RESNICK: Speaking of creation, Bertrand Russell once remarked that telling a child that "God made you" implied another question, which is "Who made God?"

GOD: That Bertie! What a card!

RESNICK: Then you don't mind if I ask it?

GOD: Ask what?

RESNICK: Who made you?

GOD: I just *hate* questions like that. And by the way, how come your name is all in caps, just like mine?

RESNICK: I'm tape-recording this. How did you know my name would be in caps?

GOD: I'm God, remember?

Resnick: No offense intended.

GOD: That's better.

Resnick: So tell me about the Big Bang.

GOD: It happened very fast. If you blinked, you'd have missed it.

Resnick: That's *it*? That's all you've got to say about it?

GOD: What do you want? No one invented the Polaroid camera for another fifteen billion years.

Resnick: If you're God, you could have invented it any time.

GOD: And if you're so smart, you could have bought Polaroid at eight and a quarter.

Resnick: What was here before the Big Bang?

GOD: Everything. But it was all kind of scrunched up. You know how it takes you a pair of nine-hour plane trips to get to Kenya? Back then you could have made it in a nannosecond. Well, maybe two nannoseconds.

Resnick: Why did you create the universe?

GOD: Beats the hell out of me.

Resnick: How can you forget? After all, you're *God*!

GOD: That's me—mysterious, unfathomable, unknowable. It can be quite a strain at times.

Resnick: By the way, is there something else I should be calling you?

GOD: Like what?

Resnick: Isn't your name YHWH?

GOD: You're kidding, right? How do you pronounce a name with no vowels (unless you're light-heavyweight champion Bobby Czyz, and there have been nights even *he* couldn't pronounce it after getting punched in the head for ten or twelve rounds.)

Resnick: Well, they say it's pronounced Yahweh—but they also say that anyone who utters it will be destroyed.

GOD: Silliest thing I ever heard.

Resnick: Then it's not true?

GOD: Not a bit of it. I see what happened: they screwed it up translating it from Aramaic to Greek to Latin and then into English.

Resnick: So people can call you Yahweh without being destroyed?

GOD: Of course. Yahweh I don't mind at all. Call me *Chubby* and I'll destroy you.

Resnick: Like you destroyed Sodom and Gomorrah?

GOD: That's right—blame *me* because they had substandard building codes.

Resnick: What about the flood?

GOD: I give up. What *about* the flood?

Resnick: Why did you cause it?

GOD: How do I know? It was a long time ago. Maybe I was having a bad hair day.

Resnick: You're not being very responsive.

GOD: You're asking too many negative questions. Ask something positive.

Resnick: Okay. What are Man's three greatest accomplishments?

GOD: Let me see...Well, the discovery of fire has to be one. And I think I'd have to say the Renaissance—I mean, Leonardo and Michelangelo and that whole crowd. And the third would be the Designated Hitter rule.

Resnick: You're kidding!

GOD: I never joke. But okay, you don't like my answer, I'm not gonna argue. Substitute the flush toilet for the Renaissance.

Resnick: Moving right along, I've got a question that I think is on many of our readers' minds these days.

GOD: One of the usual, I suppose?

Resnick: The usual?

GOD: Why do all the elevators arrive at once? Why can't any adults open a childproof bottle? How come there was an Upper Volta but there was never a Lower Volta? One of those.

Resnick: No, as a matter of fact, it wasn't any of those. But now that you mention it, why *wasn't* there a Lower Volta?

GOD: You know, I got so tired of hearing that one, I changed Upper Volta's name to Burkina Faso. Now, what was your question?

Resnick: You're God, right? Perfection personified. So how did you manage to create both Richard Nixon and Bill Clinton?

GOD: Give me a break. Do *you* win a Hugo for every story you write?

Resnick: No, but...

GOD: Besdies, do you think it was just Nixon and Clinton? Everyone's flawed.

Resnick: Everyone?

GOD: Name one that isn't.

Resnick: How about Albert Einstein?

GOD: Einstein couldn't make a free throw to save his life.

Resnick: Madam Curie.

GOD: Do you know how many times she trumped her partner's ace?

Resnick: Sophia Loren.

GOD: Okay, you got me. But *most* of my creations are flawed.

Resnick: Why, if you're God?

GOD: If you wrote the perfect book, would you ever write another?

Resnick: I don't know.

GOD: Neither do I. But I have a feeling I wouldn't. After all, I made five Marx Brothers and all those damned Kennedys, but I only made one Sophia Loren. What a dish!

Resnick: That hardly sounds godly.

GOD: I can't admire a pretty girl? Hell, I created every pretty girl you ever saw.

Resnick: Well, as long as you brought up the subject, what was Mary like?

GOD: I had an inappropriate relationship with her, and that's all I'm going to say.

Resnick: An inappropriate relationship?

GOD: Yeah, that's a legally accurate description.

Resnick: People have been arguing for 2,000 years about whether Jesus was your son or not. Maybe you can clear that up?

GOD: They didn't have DNA testing back then, did they?

Resnick: No.

GOD: Then go talk to my lawyer. I have nothing further to say on the subject. Now, have you got any more questions before I leave?

Resnick: Have you any words of wisdom for our readers?

GOD: Of course I do. I'm God.

Resnick: So what's your advice?

GOD: Never draw to an inside straight. Never bet a front-runner who's moving up in class on a muddy track. Watch out for overly-aggressive redheads name Thelma. And always go to your basement during a tornado watch.

Resnick: That's *it*? God comes down for the first time in thousands of years, and that's all you've got to tell your people?

GOD: Okay, what the hell, I'll give you one more: buy low, sell high, and stay out of commodities unless you can afford to take some heavy losses.

Resnick: Thanks. I guess.

GOD: You're welcome.

Resnick: I'll see you around.

GOD: Fat chance.

Resnick: I didn't mean in this life.

GOD: Neither did I.

## Introduction to "The 43 Antarean Dynasties"

We were in Cairo in 1989, and had a guide named Iman. He was a very pleasant, non-aggressive, intelligent fellow, who explained that he had previously taught at the university, but he made more money from tourists' tips. He told us that you couldn't even apply for a job as a guide until you had the equivalent of a Masters Degree in Egyptian History and spoke at least 4 languages fluently—which meant that he was *far* better-educated than 99% of the people he guided.

So here was this man, whose race had built pyramids and temples on an unbelievably vast scale when our ancestors were living in mud huts, showing off the lost glories of his people to the newest set of conquerors. For tips. And I remember that at one point he told us how pleased he was to have an attentive group like ours, because the last group got annoyed with him for interrupting their discussion of the point spread in the upcoming Steelers-Rams game.

I took some notes, thought about it for eight years, and wrote "The 43 Antarean Dynasties".

It won the 1998 Hugo for Best Short Story.

# THE 43 ANTAREAN DYNASTIES

*To thank the Maker Of All Things for the birth of his first male offspring, the Emperor Maloth IV ordered his architects to build a temple that would forever dwarf all other buildings on the planet. It was to be made entirely of crystal, and the spire-covered roof, which looked like a million glistening spear-points aimed at the sun, would be supported by 217 columns, to honor his 217 forebears. When struck, each column would sound a musical note that could be heard for kilometers, calling the faithful to prayer.*

*The structure would be known as the Temple of the Honored Sun, for his heir had been born exactly at midday, when the sun was highest in the sky. The temple took 27 Standard years to complete, and although races from all across the galaxy would come to Antares III to marvel at it, Maloth further decreed that no aliens or non-believers would ever be allowed to enter it and desecrate its sacred corridors with their presence...*

A man, a woman, and a child emerge from the Temple of the Honored Sun. The woman holds a camera to her eye, capturing the same image from a dozen unimaginative angles. The child, his lip sparsely covered with hair that is supposed to imply maturity, never sees beyond the game he is playing on his pocket computer. The man looks around to make sure no one is watching him, grinds out a smokeless cigar beneath his heel, and then increases his pace until he joins them.

They approach me, and I will myself to become one with my surroundings, to insinuate myself into the marble walls and stone walkways before they can speak to me.

*I am invisible. You cannot see me. You will pass me by.*

"Hey, fella—we're looking for a guide," says the man. "You interested?"

I stifle a sigh and bow deeply. "I am honored," I say, glad that they do not understand the subtleties of Antarean inflection.

"Wow!" exclaims the woman, aiming her camera at me. "I never saw anything like that! It's almost as if you folded your torso in half! Can you do it again?"

I am reminded of an ancient legend, possibly aprocryphal though I choose to believe it. An ambassador who was equally fascinated by the way the Antarean body is jointed, once asked Komarith I, the founder of the 38th Dynasty, to bow a second time. Komarith merely stared at him without moving until the embarrassed ambassador slunk away. He went on to rule for 29 years and was never known to bow again.

It has been a long time since Komarith, almost seven millennia now, and Antares and the universe have changed. I bow for the woman while she snaps her holographs.

"What's your name?" asks the man.

"You could not pronounce it," I reply. "When I conduct members of your race, I choose the name Hermes."

"Herman, eh?"

"Hermes," I correct him.

"Right. Herman."

The boy finally looks up. "He said Hermes, Dad."

The man shrugs. "Whatever." He looks at his timepiece. "Well, let's get started."

"Yeah," chimes in the child. "They're piping in the game from Roosevelt III this afternoon. I've got to get back for it."

"You can watch sports anytime," says the woman. "This may be your only chance to see Antares."

"I should be so lucky," he mutters, returning his attention to his computer.

I recite my introductory speech almost by rote. "Allow me to welcome you to Antares III, and to its capital city of Kalimetra, known throughout the galaxy as the City of a Million Spires."

"I didn't see any million spires when we took the shuttle in from the spaceport," says the child, whom I could have sworn was not listening. "A thousand or two, maybe."

"There was a time when there were a million," I explain. "Today only 16,304 remain. Each is made of quartz or crystal. In late afternoon, when the sun sinks low in the sky, they act as a prism for its rays, creating a flood of exotic colors that stretches across the thoroughfares of the city. Races have come from halfway across the galaxy to experience the effect."

"Sixteen thousand," murmurs the woman. "I wonder what happened to the rest?"

*No one knew why Antareans found the spires so aesthetically pleasing. They towered above the cities, casting their shadows and their shifting colors across the landscape. Tall, delicate, exquisite, they reflected a unique grandness of vision and sensitivity of spirit. The rulers of Antares III spent almost 38,000 years constructing their million spires.*

*During the Second Invasion, it took the Canphorite armada less than two weeks to destroy all but 16,304 of them...*

The woman is still admiring the spires that she can see in the distance. Finally she asks who built them, as if they are too beautiful to have been created by Antareans.

"The artisans and craftsmen of my race built everything you will see today," I answer.

"All by yourselves?"

"Is it so difficult for you to believe?" I ask gently.

"No," she says defensively. "Of course not. It's just that there's so *much*..."

"Kalimetra was not created in a day or a year, or even a millennium," I point out. "It is the cumulative achievement of 43 Antarean Dynasties."

"So we're in the 43rd Dynasty now?" she asks.

*It was Zelorean IX who officially declared Kalimetra to be the Eternal City. Neither war nor insurrection had ever threatened its stability, and even the towering temples of his forefathers gave every promise of lasting for all eternity. It was a Golden Age, and he could see no reason why it should not go on forever...*

"The last absolute ruler of the 43rd Dynasty has been dust for almost three thousand years," I explain. "Since then we have been governed by a series of conquerers, each alien race superceding the last."

"Thank goodness they didn't destroy your buildings," says the woman, turning to admire a water fountain, which for some reason appears to her to be a mystical alien artifact. She is about to take a holo when the child restrains her.

"It's just a goddamned water bubbler, Ma," he says.

"But it's fascinating," she says. "Imagine what kind of beings used it in ages past."

"Thirsty ones," says the bored child.

She ignores him and turns back to me. "As I was saying, it must be criminal to rob the galaxy of such treasures."

"Yeah, well *somebody* destroyed some buildings around here," interjects the child, who seems intent on proving someone wrong about something. "Remember the hole in the ground we saw over that way?" He points in the direction of the Footprint. "Looks like a bomb crater to me."

"You are mistaken," I explain, leading them over to it. "It has always been there."

"It's just a big sinkhole," says the man, totally unimpressed.

"It is worshipped by my people as the Footprint of God," I explain. "Once, many eons ago, Kalimetra was in the throes of a years-long drought. Finally Jorvash, our greatest priest, offered his own life if God would bring the rains. God replied that it would not rain until He wept again, and we had not yet suffered enough to bring forth His tears of compassion. But He promised that He would strike a bargain with Jorvash." I pause for effect, but the man is lighting another cigar and the child is concentrating on his pocket computer. "The next morning Jorvash was found dead inside his temple, while God had created this depression with His foot and filled it with water. It sustained us until He finally wept again."

The woman seems flustered. "Um...I hate to ask," she finally says, "but could you repeat that story? My recorder wasn't on."

The man looks uncomfortable. "She's always forgetting to turn the damned thing on," he explains, and flips me a coin. "For your trouble."

*Lobilia was the greatest poet in the history of Antares III. Although he died during the 23rd Dynasty, most of his work survived him. But his masterpiece, "The Long Night of the Exile" —the epic of Bagata's Exile and his triumphant Return—was lost forever.*

*Though he was his race's most famous bard, Lobilia himself was illiterate, unable even to write his own name. He created his poetry extemporaneously, embellishing upon it with each retelling. He recited his epic just once, and was so satisfied with its form that he refused to repeat it for the scribes who were waiting for a final version and hadn't written it down.*

"Thank you," says the woman, deactivating the recorder after I finish. She pauses. "Can I buy a book with some more of your quaint folk legends?"

I decide not to explain the difference between a folk legend and an article of belief. "They are for sale in the gift shop of your hotel," I reply.

"You don't have enough books?" mutters the man.

She glares at him, but says nothing, and I lead them to the Tomb, which always impresses visitors.

"This is the Tomb of Bedorian V, the greatest ruler of the 37th Dynasty," I say. "Bedorian was a commoner, a simple farmer who deposed the notorious Maelastri XII, himself a mighty warrior who was the last ruler of the 36th Dynasty. It was Bedorian who decreed universal education for all Antareans."

"What did you have before that?"

"Our females were not allowed the privilege of literacy until Bedorian's reign."

"How did this guy finally die?" asks the man, who doesn't really care but is unwilling to let the woman ask all the questions.

"Bedorian was assassinated by one of his followers," I reply.

"A male, no doubt," says the woman wryly.

"Before he died," I continue, "he united three warring states without fighting a single battle, decreed that all Antareans should use a common language, and outlawed the worship of *kreneks*."

"What are *kreneks*?"

"They are poisonous reptiles. They killed many worshippers in nameless, obscene ceremonies before Bedorian IV came to power."

"Yeah?" says the child, alert again. "What were they like?"

"What is obscene to one being is simply boring to another," I say. "Terrans find them dull." Which is not true, but I have no desire to watch the child snicker as I describe the rituals.

"What a shame," says the woman, though her voice sounds relieved. "Still, you certainly seem to know your history."

I want to answer that I just make up the stories. But I am afraid if I say it, she will believe it.

"Where did you learn all this stuff?" she continues.

"To become a licensed guide," I reply, "an Antarean must undergo fourteen years of study, and must also speak a minimum of four alien languages fluently. Terran is always one of the four."

"That's some set of credentials," comments the man. "I made it through one year of dental school and quit."

*And yet, it is you who are paying me.*

"I'm surprised you don't work at one of the local universities," he continues.

"I did once."

Which is true. But I have my family to feed—and tourists' tips, however small and grudgingly given, are still greater than my salary as a teacher.

A *rapu*—an Antarean child—insinuates his way between myself and my clients. Scarcely more than an infant, he is dressed in rags, and his face is smudged with dirt. There are open sores on the reticulated plates of his skin, and his golden eyes water constantly. He begs plaintively for credits in his native tongue. When there is no response, he extends his hand in what has become a universal gesture that says: *You are rich. I am poor and hungry. Give me money.*

"Yours?" asks the man, frowning, as his wife takes half a dozen holos in quick succession.

"No, he is not mine."

"What is he doing here?"

"He lives in the street," I answer, my compassion for the *rapu* alternating with my humilation at having to explain his presence and situation. "He is asking for coins so that he and his mother will not go hungry tonight."

I look at the *rapu* and think sadly: *Timing is everything. Once, long ago, we strode across our world like gods. You would not have gone hungry in any of the 43 Dynasties.*

The human child looks at his Antarean counterpart. I wonder if he realizes how fortunate he is. His face gives no reflection of his thoughts; perhaps he has none. Finally he picks his nose and goes back to manipulating his computer.

The man stares at the *rapu* for a moment, then flips him a two-credit coin. The *rapu* catches it, bows and blesses the man, and runs off. We watch him go. He raises the coin above his head, yelling happily—and a moment later, we are surrounded by twenty more street urchins, all filthy, all hungry, all begging for coins.

"Enough's enough!" says the man irritably. "Tell them to get the hell out of here and go home, Herman."

"They live here," I explain gently.

"Right here?" demands the man. He stomps the ground with his foot, and the nearest *rapus* jump back in fright. "On this spot? Okay, then tell them to stay here where they live and not follow us."

I explain to the *rapus* in our own tongue that these tourists will not give them coins.

"Then we will go to the ugly pink hotel where all the Men stay and rob their rooms."

"That is none of my concern," I say. "But if you are caught, it will go hard with you."

The oldest of the urchins smiles at my warning.

"If we are caught, they will lock us up, and because it is a jail they will have to feed us, and we will be protected from the rain and the cold—it is far better than being here."

I have no answer for *rapus* whose only ambition is to be warm and dry and well-fed, but merely shrug. They run off, laughing and singing, as if they are human children off to play some game.

"Damned aliens!" mutters the man.

"That is incorrect," I say.

"Oh?"

"A matter of semantics," I point out gently. "*They* are indigenous. *You* are the aliens."

"Well, they could do with some lessons in behavior from us aliens, then," he growls.

We walk up the long ramp to the Tomb and are about to enter it, when the woman stops.

"I'd like a holo of the three of you standing in the entrance," she announces. She smiles at me. "Just to prove to our friends we were here, and that we met a real Antarean."

The man walks over and stands on one side of me. The child reluctantly moves to my other side.

"Now put your arm around Herman," says the woman.

The child steps back, and I see a mixture of contempt and disgust on his face. "I'll pose with it, but I won't *touch* it!"

"You do what your mother says!" snaps the man.

"No way!" says the child, stalking sulkily back down the ramp. "You want to hug him, you go ahead!"

"You listen to me, young man!" says the man, but the child does not stop or give any indication that he has heard, and soon he disappears behind a temple.

*It was Tcharock, the founder of the 30th Dynasty, who decreed that the person of the Emperor was sacrosanct and could not be touched by any being other than his medics and his concubines, and then only with his consent.*

*His greatest advisor was Chaluba, who extended Tcharock's rule to more than 80% of the planet and halted the hyper-inflation that had been the 29th Dynasty's legacy to him.*

*One night, during a state function, Chaluba inadvertantly brushed against Tcharock while introducing him to the Ambassador from far Domar.*

*The next morning Tcharock regretfully gave the signal to the executioner, and Chaluba was beheaded. Despite this unfortunate beginning, the 30th Dynasty survived for 1,062 Standard years.*

The woman, embarrassed, begins apologizing to me. But I notice that she, too, avoids touching me. The man goes off after the child, and a few moments later the two of them return—which is just as well, for the woman has begun repeating herself.

The man pushes the child toward me, and he sullenly utters an apology. The man takes an ominous step toward him, and he reluctantly reaches out his hand. I take it briefly—the contact is no more pleasant for me than for him—and then we enter the Tomb. Two other groups are there, but they are hundreds of meters away, and we cannot hear what their guides are saying.

"How high is the ceiling?" asks the woman, training her camera on the exquisite carvings overhead.

"38 meters," I say. "The Tomb itself is 203 meters long and 67 meters wide. The body of Beldorian V is in a large vault beneath the floor." I pause, thinking as always of past glories. "On the Day of Mourning, the day the Tomb was completed, a million Antareans stood patiently in line outside the Tomb to pay their last respects."

"I don't mean to ask a silly question," says the woman, "but why are all the buildings so *enormous*?"

"Ego," suggests the man, confident in his wisdom.

"The Maker Of All Things is huge," I explain. "So my people felt that any monuments to Him should be as large as possible, so that He might be comfortable inside them."

"You think your God can't find or fit into a small building?" asks the man with a condescending smile.

"He is everyone's God," I answer. "And while He can of course find a small temple, why should we force Him to live in one?"

"Did Beldorian have a wife?" asks the woman, her mind back to smaller considerations.

"He had five of them," I answer. "The tomb next to this one is known as The Place of Beldorian's Queens."

"He was a polygamist?"

I shake my head. "No. Beldorian simply outlived his first four queens."

"He must have died a very old man," says the woman.

"He did not," I answer. "There is a belief among my people that those who achieve public greatness are doomed to private misery. Such was Beldorian's fate." I turn to the child, who has been silent since returning, and ask him if he has any questions, but he merely glares at me without speaking.

"How long ago was this place built?" asks the man.

"Beldorian V died 6,302 Standard years ago. It took another 17 years to build and prepare the Tomb."

"6,302 years," he muses. "That's a long time."

"We are an ancient race," I reply proudly. "A human anthropologist has suggested that our 3rd Dynasty commenced before your ancestors crossed over the evolutionary barrier into sentience."

"Maybe we spent a long time living in the trees," says the man, clearly unimpressed and just a bit defensive. "But look how quickly we passed you once we climbed down."

"If you say so," I answer noncommittally.

"In fact, everybody passed you," he persists. "Look at the record: How many times has Antares been conquered?"

"I am not sure," I lie, for I find it humiliating to speak of it.

*When the Antareans learned that Man's Republic wish to annex their world, they gathered their army in Zanthu and then marched out onto the battlefield, 300,000 strong. They were the cream of the planet's young warriors, gold of eye, the reticulated plates of their skin glistening in the morning sun, prepared to defend their homeworld.*

*The Republic sent a single ship that flew high overhead and dropped a single bomb, and in less than a second there was no longer an Antarean army, or a city of Zanthu, or a Great Library of Cthstoka.*

*Over the millennia Antares was conquered four times by Man, twice by the Canphor Twins, and once each by Lodin XI, Emra, Ramor, and the Sett Empire. It was said that the parched ground had finally quenched its thirst by drinking a lake of Antarean blood.*

As we leave the Tomb, we come to a small, skinny *rapu*. He sits on a rock, staring at us with his large, golden eyes, his expression rapt in contemplation.

The human child pointedly ignores him and continues walking toward the next temple, but the adults stop.

"What a cute little thing!" enthuses the woman. "And he looks so hungry." She digs into her shoulder bag and withdraws a sweet that she has kept from breakfast. "Here," she says, holding it up. "Would you like it?"

The *rapu* never moves. This is unique not only in the woman's experience, but also in mine, for he is obviously undernourished.

"Maybe he can't metabolize it," suggests the man. He pulls a coin out, steps over to the *rapu*, and extends his hand. "Here you go, kid."

The *rapu*, his face frozen in contemplation, makes no attempt to grab the coin.

And suddenly I am thinking excitedly: *You disdain their food when you are hungry, and their money when you are poor. Could you possibly be the One we have awaited for so many millennia, the One who will give us back our former glory and initiate the 44th Dynasty?*

I study him intently, and my excitement fades just as quickly as it came upon me. The *rapu* does not disdain their food and their money. His golden eyes are clouded over. Life in the streets has so weakened him that he has become blind, and of course he does not understand what they are saying. His seeming arrogance comes not from pride or some inner light, but because he is not aware of their offerings.

"Please," I say, gently taking the sweet from the woman without coming into actual contact with her fingers. I walk over and place it in the *rapu's* hand. He sniffs it, then gulps it down hungrily and extends his hand, blindly begging for more.

"It breaks your heart," says the woman.

"Oh, it's no worse than what we saw on Bareimus V," responds the man. "They were every bit as poor—and remember that awful skin disease that they all had?"

The woman considers, and her face reflects the unpleasantness of the memory. "I suppose you're right at that." She shrugs, and I can tell that even though the child is still in front of us, hand outstretched, she has already put him from her mind.

I lead them through the Garden of the Vanished Princes, with its tormented history of sacrifice and intrigue, and suddenly the man stops.

"What happened here?" he asks, pointing to a number of empty pedestals.

"History happened," I explain. "Or avarice, for sometimes they are the same thing." He seems confused, so I continue: "If any of our conquerers could find a way to transport a treasure back to his home planet, he did. Anything small enough to be plundered *was* plundered."

"And these statues that have been defaced?" he says, pointing to them. "Did you do it yourselves so they would be worthless to occupying armies?"

"No," I answer.

"Well, whoever did *that*"—he points to a headless statue —"ought to be strung up and whipped."

"What's the fuss?" asks the child in a bored voice. "They're just statues of aliens."

"Actually, the human who did that was rewarded with the governorship of Antares III," I inform them.

"What are you talking about?" says the man.

"The second human conquest of the Antares system was led by Commander Lois Kiboko," I begin. "She defaced or destroyed more than 3,000 statues. Many were physical representations of our deity, and since she and her crew were devout believers in one of your religions, she felt that these were false idols and must be destroyed."

"Well," the man replies with a shrug, "it's a small price to pay for her saving you from the Lodinites."

"Perhaps," I say. "The problem is that we had to pay a greater price for each successive savior."

He stares at me, and there is an awkward silence. Finally I suggest that we visit the Palace of the Supreme Tyrant.

"You seem such a docile race," she says awkwardly. "I mean, so civilized and unaggressive. How did your gene pool ever create a real, honest-to-goodness tyrant?"

The truth is that our gene pool was considerably more aggressive before a seemingly endless series of alien conquests decimated it. But I know that this answer would make them uncomfortable, and could affect the size of my tip, so I lie to them instead. (I am ashamed to admit that lying to aliens becomes easier with each passing day. Indeed, I am sometimes amazed at the facility with which I can create falsehoods.)

"Every now and then each race produces a genetic sport," I say, and I can see she believes it, "and we Antareans are so docile, to use your expression, that this particular one had no difficulty achieving power."

"What was his name?"

"I do not know."

"I thought you took fourteen years' worth of history courses," she says accusingly, and I can tell she thinks I am lying to her, whereas every time I have actually lied she has believed me.

"Our language has many dialects, and they have all evolved and changed over 36,000 years," I point out. "Some we have deciphered, but to this day many of them remain unsolved mysteries. In fact, right at this moment a team of human archaeologists is hard at work trying to uncover the Tyrant's name."

"If it's a dead language, how are they going to manage that?"

"In the days when your race was still planetbound, there was an artifact called the Rosetta Stone that helped you translate an ancient language. We have something similar—ours is known as the Bosperi Scroll—that comes from the Great Tyrant's era."

"Where is it?" asks the woman, looking around.

"I regret to inform you that both the archaeologists and the Bosperi Scroll are currently in a museum on Deluros VIII."

"Smart," says the man. "They can protect it better on Deluros."

"From who?" asks the woman.

"From anyone who wants to steal it, of course," he says, as if explaining it to a child.

"But I mean, who would want to steal the key to a dead language?"

"Do you know what it would be worth to a collector?" answers the man. "Or a thief who wanted to ransom it?"

They discuss it further, but the simple truth is that it is on Deluros because it was small enough to carry, and for no other reason. When they are through arguing I tell her that it is because they have devices on Deluros that will bring back the faded script, and she nods her head thoughtfully.

We walk another 400 kilometers and come to the immense Palace of the Kings. It is made entirely of gold, and becomes so hot from the rays of the sun that one can touch the outer surface only at night. This was the building in which all the rulers of the 7th through the 12th Dynasties resided. It was from here that my race received the Nine Proclamations of Ascendency, and the Charter of Universal Rights, and our most revered document, the Mabelian Declaration.

It was a wondrous time to have lived, when we had never tasted defeat and all problems were capable of solution, when stately caravans plied their trade across secure boundaries and monarchs were just and wise, when each day brought new triumphs and the future held infinite promise.

I point to the broken and defaced stone chair. "Once there were 246 jewels and precious stones embedded in the throne."

The child walks over to the throne, then looks at me accusingly. "Where are they?" he demands.

"They were all stolen over the millennia," I reply.

"By conquerers, of course," offers the woman with absolute certainty.

"Yes," I say, but again I am lying. They were stolen by my own people, who traded them to various occupying armies for food or the release of captive loved ones.

We spend a few more minutes examining the vanished glory of the Palace of the Kings, then walk out the door and approach the next crumbling structure. It is the Hall of the Thinkers, revered to this day by all Antareans, but I know they will not understand why a race would create such an ediface to scholarship, and I haven't the energy to explain, so I tell them that it is the Palace of the Concubines, and of course they believe me. At one point the child, making no attempt to mask his disappointment, asks why there are no statues or carvings showing the concubines, and I think very quickly and explain that Lois Kiboko's religious beliefs were offended by the sexual frankness of the artifacts and she had them all destroyed.

I feel guilty about this lie, for it is against the Code of Just Behavior to suggest that a visitor's race may have offended in any way. Ironically, while the child voices his disappointment, I notice that none of the three seems to have a problem accepting that another human would destroy millennia-old artwork that upset his sensibilities. I decide that since they feel no guilt, this one time I shall feel none either. (But I still do. Tradition is a difficult thing to transcend.)

I see the man anxiously walking around, looking into corners and behind pedestals, and I ask him if something is wrong.

"Where's the can?" he says.

"I beg your pardon?"

"The can. The bathroom. The lavatory." He frowns. "Didn't any of these goddamned concubines ever have to take a crap?"

I finally discern what he wants and direct him to a human facility that has been constructed just beyond the Western Door.

He returns a few minutes later, and I lead them all outside, past the towering Onyx Obelisk that marked the beginning of the almost-forgotten 4th Dynasty. We stop briefly at the Temple of the River of Light, which was constructed *over* the river, so that the sacred waters flow through the temple itself.

We leave and turn a corner, and suddenly a single structure completely dominates the landscape.

"What's *that*?" asks the woman.

"That is the Spiral Ramp to Heaven," I answer.

"What a fabulous name!" she enthuses. "I just know a fabulous story goes with it!" She turns to me expectantly.

"There was a time, before our scientists knew better, that people thought you could reach heaven if you simply built a tall enough ramp."

The child guffaws.

"It is true," I continue. "Construction was begun during the 2nd Dyntasy, and continued for more than 700 years until midway through the 3rd. It looks as if you can see the top from here, but you actually are looking only at the bottom half of it. The rest is obscured by clouds."

"How high does it go?" asked the woman.

"More than nine kilometers," I say. "Three kilometers higher than our tallest mountain."

"Amazing!" she exclaims.

"Perhaps you would like a closer look at it?" I suggest. "You might even wish to climb the first kilometer. It is a very gentle ascent until you reach the fifth kilometer."

"Yes," she replies happily. "I think I'd like that very much."

"I'm not climbing anything," says the man.

"Oh, come on," she urges him. "It'll be fun!"

"The air's too thin and the gravity's too heavy and it's too damned much like work. One of these days *I'm* going to choose our itinerary, and I promise you it won't involve so goddamned much walking."

"Can we go back and watch the game?" asks the child eagerly.

The man takes one more look at the Spiral Ramp to Heaven. "Yeah," he says. "I've seen enough. Let's go back."

"We really should finish the tour," says the woman. "We'll probably never be in this sector of the galaxy again."

"So what? It's just another backwater world," replies the man. "Don't tell your friends about the Stairway to the Stars or whatever the hell it's called and they'll never know you missed it."

Then the woman comes up with what she imagines will be the clinching argument. "But you've already agreed to pay for the tour."

"So we'll cut it short and pay him half as much," says the man. "Big deal."

The man pulls a wad of credits out of his pocket and peels off three ten-credits notes. Then he pauses, looks at me, pockets them, and presses a fifty-credit note into my hand instead.

"Ah, hell, you kept your end of the bargain, Herman," he says. Then he and the woman and child begin walking back to the hotel.

*The first aliens ever to visit Antares were rude and ill-mannered barbarians, but Perganian II, the greatest Emperor of the 26th Dynasty, decreed that they must be treated with the utmost courtesy. When the day of their departure finally arrived, the aliens exchanged farewells with Perganian, and one of them thrust a large, flawless blue diamond into the Emperor's hand in payment for his hospitality.*

*After the aliens left the courtyard, Perganian let the diamond drop to the ground, declaring that no Antarean could be purchased for any price.*

*The diamond lay where it had fallen for three generations, becoming a holy symbol of Antarean dignity and independence. It finally vanished during a dust storm and was never seen again.*

## Introduction to "Roots...and a Few Vines"

Some writers were never a part of science fiction fandom. Others leave it as soon as they turn pro.

Not me. I was, am, and always will be a science fiction fan. Writing is my profession; fandom is my life.

I expressed words to that effect at a Midwestcon a few years ago, and Rich Lynch, co-editor with his wife Nikki of the multiple-Hugo-winning fanzine *Mimosa,* asked me to write an article about it.

So I did. It appeared in *Mimosa* in this form, and because I hate for anything I write to appear just once and/or not make money, I sold a somewhat shorter version of it to *Science Fiction Age.*

# ROOTS AND A FEW VINES

So I'm sitting there in Winnipeg, resplendent in my tuxedo, and morbidly wondering how many fans have called me "Mr. Resnick" instead of "Mike" since the worldcon began three days ago.

I don't *feel* like a Mister. I feel like a fan who is cheating by sitting here with all the pros, waiting for Bob Silverberg to announce the winner of the Best Editor Hugo. He goes through the names: Datlow, Dozois, Resnick, Rusch, Schmidt.

He opens the envelope and reads off Kris Rusch's name, and suddenly I am walking up to the stage. Bob is sure I thought he called out *my* name, and looks like he is considering clutching the Hugo to his breast and running off with it (although that is actually a response common to all pros when they are in proximity to a Hugo), but finally he sighs and hands it over to me, and I start thanking Ed Ferman and all the voters.

What am I doing here, I wonder, picking up a Hugo for a lady who is half my age and has twice my talent and is drop-dead gorgeous to boot? How in blazes did I ever get to be an Elder Statesman?

* * *

Well, it began in 1962, which, oddly enough, was *not* just last year, no matter how it feels. Carol and I had met at the University of Chicago in 1960. We'd gone to the theater on our first date, and wound up in the Morrison Hotel's coffee shop, where we talked science fiction until they threw us out at 5 in the morning. It was the first time either of us realized that someone else out there read that crazy Buck Rogers stuff (though we might have guessed, since they continued to print it month after month, and two sales per title would hardly seem enough to keep the publishers in business.)

Well, 1962 rolls around, and so does a future Campbell winner named Laura...but the second biggest event of the year comes when Ace Books, under the editorship of Don Wollheim, starts pirating a bunch of Edgar Rice Burroughs novels, and a whole generation gets to learn about Tarzan and Frank Frazetta and John Carter and Roy Krenkal and David Innes all at once.

But the important thing, the thing that unquestionably shaped my adult life, was that one of the books had a little blurb on the inside front cover extolling ERB's virtues, and it was signed "Camille Cazedessus, Editor of *ERB-dom*". Well, you didn't have to be a genius to figure out that *ERB-dom*, at least in that context, was an obvious reference to Edgar Rice Burroughs.

A whole magazine devoted to one of my favorite writers? I could barely wait until the next morning, when I took the subway downtown and entered the Post Office News, Chicago's largest magazine store. I looked for *ERB-dom* next to *Time, Life, Look, Newsweek,* and *Playboy.* Wasn't there. I looked for it next to *Analog, Galaxy,* and *F&SF.* No dice. Wasn't anywhere near *Forbes* or *Fortune* or *Business Week* either.

So I go up to the manager and tell him I'm looking for *ERB-dom*, and he checks his catalogs and tells me there ain't no such animal.

I grab him by the arm, drag him over to the paperbacks, pull out the operative Burroughs title, turn to the inside front cover, and smite him with a mighty *"Aha!"*

So he promises to get cracking and find out who publishes this magazine and start stocking it, and I return to our subterranean penthouse (i.e., basement apartment) to await the Good News.

Which doesn't come.

I nag Post Office News incessantly. I nag my local bookstore. I nag the public library. I even nag my mother. (This seems counter-productive, but she has been nagging *me* for 20 years and fair is fair.)

Finally, I look at my watch and it is half-past 1962 and there is still no sign of *ERB-dom*, so I write to the editor, Miss Cazedessus (so okay, until then I'd never heard of a *guy* named Camille), in care of Ace Books, and a month later the first five issues of *ERB-dom* arrive in the mail, the very first fanzines I have ever seen, along with a long, friendly letter that constantly uses the arcane word "worldcon".

Within two months I have written three long articles for *ERB-dom #6* and have become its associate editor. There is a worldcon in Chicago that summer, not a 20-minute subway ride from where we live, but the future Campbell winner chooses August 17 to get herself born, and we do not go to the worldcon. When she is 8 days old I decide to forgive her and lovingly show her off to her grandparents, and she vomits down the back of my Hawaiian shirt (which, in retrospect, could well have been an editorial comment), and it is 27 years before I willingly touch her again, but that is another story.

There is one other thing that happens in 1962. We are living at the corner of North Shore and Greenview in the Rogers Park area of Chicago, and right across street of us is this old apartment building, and on the third Saturday of every month strange-looking men and women congregate there. They have long hair, and most of them are either 90 pounds overweight or 50 pounds underweight, and often they are carrying books under their arms. We decide they are members of SNCC or CORE, which are pretty popular organizations at the time, and that they are meeting there to figure out how to dodge the draft, and that the books they carry are either pacifist tracts or ledgers with the names and addresses of all the left-wing groups that have contributed money to them.

We have to go all the way to Washington D.C. a year later and attend Discon I to find out that they are not draft dodgers (well, not *primarily*, anyway) but rather Chicago fandom, and that they have been meeting 80 feet from our front door for 2 years.

* * *

So I wend my way back through the audience, and I find my seat, and I hand Kris Rusch's Hugo to Carol, because I am also up for Best Short Story, and I think I've got a better chance at this, and when I run up to accept the award it will look tacky to already be carrying a Hugo. Besides, Charles Sheffield is sitting right next to us, and he is up for Best Novelette, and he is getting very nervous, and wants to stroke the Hugo for luck, or maybe is considering just walking out with it and changing the name plates at a future date. (In fact, I am convinced that if he does not win his own, neither Kris nor I will ever see *her* Hugo again. Charles will probably deny this, but never forget that Charles gets paid an inordinate amount of money to tell lies to the public at large.)

So Guy Gavriel Kay begins reading off the nominees, and suddenly I realize that I am not nervous at all, that this is becoming very old hat to me. I have been nominated for nine Hugos in the past six years. I have actually won a pair. Worldcons are very orderly things: you show up, you sign a million autographs, you eat each meal with a different editor and line up your next year's worth of work, and then you climb into your tux and see if you won another Hugo.

It's gotten to be such a regular annual routine, you sometimes find yourself idly wondering: was it *always* like this?

Then you think back to your first worldcon, and you realize that no, it was not always like this...

★ ★ ★

Right off the bat, we were the victims of false doctrine. Everyone we knew in fandom—all six or seven of them—told us the worldcon was held over Labor Day weekend. So we took them at their word.

The problem, of course, was the definition of "weekend". We took a train that pulled out of Chicago on Friday morning, and dumped us in the basement of our Washington D.C. hotel at 9:00 Saturday morning. At which time we found out that the convention was already half over.

(Things were different then. There were no times in the convention listings. In fact, there were no convention listings. Not in *Analog*, not anywhere. If you knew that worldcons even existed, you were already halfway to being a trufan.)

Caz (right: he wasn't a Miss at all) met us and showed us around. Like myself, he was dressed in a suit and tie; it was a few more worldcons before men wore shirts without jackets or ties, even during the afternoons, and every woman—they formed, at most, 10% of the attendees, and over half were writers' wives— wore a skirt. If you saw someone with a beard—a relatively rare occurrence—you knew he was either a pro writer or Bruce Pelz.

When we got to the huckster room—20-plus dealers (and selling only books, magazines, and fanzines; none of the junk that dominates the tables today), I thought I had died and gone to heaven. The art show had work by Finlay and Freas and Emsh and even Margaret Brundage; only J. Allen St. John was missing from among the handful of artists whose work I knew and admired.

They had an auction. It even had a little booklet telling you what items would be auctioned when, so you knew which session to attend to get what you wanted. Stan Vinson, a famous Burroughs collector who had been corresponding with me for a year, bought a Frazetta cover painting for $70. Friends told him he was crazy; paintings were supposed to appreciate, and no one would ever pay that much for a Frazetta again. I bought a Finlay sketch for $2.00, and an autographed Sturgeon manuscript for $3.50.

In the afternoon we decide to go to the panels. I do not know from panels; like any neo, I take along a pencil and a notebook. The panels are not what we have these days, or at least they did not seem so to my untrained and wondrous eyes and ears.

For example, there is a panel with Willy Ley and Isaac Asimov and Fritz Leiber and L. Sprague de Camp and Ed Emsh and Leigh Bracket, and the topic is "What Should a BEM Look Like?" (I have a copy of the *Discon Proceedings*, a transcript of the entire convention published by Advent, and to this day when I need a new alien race I re-read that panel and invariably I come up with one.)

There was a panel with Fred Pohl and a tyro named Budrys and a gorgeous editor (though not as gorgeous as the one I accepted a Hugo for) named Cele Goldsmith and even ***John Campbell Himself***, on how to write stories around cover paintings, which was a common practice back then, and which remains fascinating reading today.

There was a sweet old guy in a white suit who saw that we were new to all this, and moseyed over and spent half an hour with us, making us feel at home and telling us about how we were all one big family and inviting us to come to all the parties at night. Then he wandered off to accept the first-ever Hall of Fame Award from First Fandom. When they asked if he was working on anything at present, he replied that he had just delivered the manuscript to *Skylark DuQuesne*, and received the second-biggest ovation I have ever heard at a worldcon. (The biggest came 30 years later, when Andy Porter broke a 12-year losing streak and won the semi-prozine Hugo in 1993.)

Since we didn't know anyone, and were really rather shy (over the years, I have learned to over-compensate for this tendency, as almost anyone will tell you, bitterly and at length,) we ate dinner alone, then watched the masquerade, which in those days was truly a masquerade ball and not a competition. There was a band, and everyone danced, and a few people showed up in costume, and every now and then one of them would march across the stage, and at the end of the ball they announced the winners.

Then there was the Bheer Blast. In those bygone days, they didn't show movies. (I think movies turned up in 1969, *not* to display the Hugo nominees or give pleasure to the cinema buffs, but to give the kids a place to sleep so they'd stop cluttering up the lobby.) They didn't give out the Hugos at night, either. (An evening banquet might run $5.00 a head, and the concom got enough grief for charging $3.00 a head for rubber chicken served at 1:00 PM rather than six hours later.) They didn't have more than one track of programming. (Multiple tracks came along 8 years later, and evening programs even later than that.)

Well, with all the things they *didn't* have, they needed a way to amuse the congoers in the evening, so what happened was this: every bid committee (and they only bid a year in advance back then) treated the entire convention to a beer party on a different night. We could all fit in one room—I know the official tally for Discon I was 600, but I was there and I'll swear that there were no more than 400 or so in attendance; the other 200 must have been no-shows, or waiters, or bellboys—and the bidding committee would treat us to a small lakeful of beer, with or without pretzels, and then the next night a rival bid would do the same thing. (You voted—if you could drag yourself out of bed—on Sunday morning at the business meeting. A fan would speak for each bid, telling you how wonderful his committee was. Then a pro would speak for each bid, telling you about the quality of restaurants you would encounter. The better restaurants invariably carried the day.)

After the beer blast was over, everyone vanished. The Burroughs people, all of them straighter than Tarzan's arrows, went to bed. We remembered that Doc Smith had mentioned parties, so we began wandering down the empty, foreboding corridors of the hotel, wondering if the parties really did exist, and how to find them.

We walked all the way down one floor, took the stairs up a flight, repeated the procedure, then did it again. We were about to quit when a door opened, and a little bearded man and a thin balding man, both with thick glasses, spotted our name badges and asked if we'd like to come in for a drink. We didn't know who the hell they were, but they had badges too, so we knew they were with the con and probably not about to mug a couple of innocents from Chicago, and we decided to join them.

Turns out they were standing in the doorway to a huge suite, and that their names were del Rey and Blish. Inside, wearing a bowtie and looking not unlike a penguin in his black suit, was Isaac Asimov. Randy Garrett was dressed in something all-satin and not of this century. Bob Silverberg looked young and incredibly dapper. Sam Moskowitz was speaking to Ed Hamilton and Leigh Brackett in a corner; this was many years before his throat surgery, and it was entirely possible, though unlikely, that no one in the basement could hear him.

*And every last one of them went out of their way to talk to us and make us feel at home.*

Later another young fan wandered in. Much younger than me. I was 21; Jack Chalker was only 19. We sat around, and discussed various things, and then something strange happened, something totally alien to my experience.

Someone asked Jack and I what we wanted to do with our lives. (No, that's not the strange part; people were always asking that.)

We each answered that we wanted to write science fiction.

And you know what? For the first time in my life, *nobody laughed*.

That's when I knew I was going to come back to worldcons for the rest of my life.

★ ★ ★

So Guy Gavriel Kay reads off the list of nominees, and then he opens the envelope, and the winner is Connie Willis, and I am second to her again for the 83rd time (yeah, I know, I've only lost 76 Hugos and Nebulas to her, but it *feels* like 83), and everyone tells me I've won a moral victory because I have beat all the short stories and Connie's winner is a novelette that David Bratman, in his infinite wisdom, decided to move to the short story category, and I keep thinking that moral victories and 60 cents will get you a cup of coffee anywhere west of New York and east of California, and that I wish I didn't like Connie so much so that I could hate her just a little on Labor Day weekends, and my brain is making up slogans, modified slightly from my youth, slogans like *Break Up Connie Willis*, which is certainly easier than breaking up the Yankees, and I am wondering if Tanya Harding will loan me her bodyguard for a few days, and then I am at the Hugo Losers Party, and suddenly it doesn't matter that I've lost a Hugo, because it is now 31 years since that first worldcon I went to, and it is my annual family reunion, and I am visiting with friends that I see once or twice or, on good years, five times per year, and we have a sense of continuity and community that goes back for almost two-thirds of my life. Hugos are very nice, and I am proud of the ones I've won, and I am even proud of the ones I've lost, but when all is said and done, they are metal objects and my friends are people, and people are what life is all about.

And I find, to my surprise, that almost everyone I am talking to, almost all the old friends I am hugging and already planning to see again at the next worldcon, are fans. Some, like me, write for a living; a few paint; most do other things. But we share a common fannish history, and a common fannish language, and common fannish interests, and I realize that I even enjoyed the business meeting this year, and you have to be pretty far gone into fandom to enjoy Ben Yalow making a point of order.

★ ★ ★

A lot of pros don't go to worldcon anymore. They prefer World Fantasy Con. It's smaller, more intimate, and it's limited to 750 members—and while this is not official, there is nonetheless a "Fans Not Wanted" sign on the door.

That's probably why I don't go. It's true that worldcons have changed, that people who read and write science fiction are probably a minority special interest group these days, that bad movies will outdraw the Hugo ceremony...but the trufans are there. It just means you have to work a little harder to hunt them up.

One of the things I have tried to do with the new writers I have helped to bring into this field, the coming superstars like Nick DiChario and Barb Delaplace and Michelle Sagara and Jack Nimersheim and all the many others, is to not only show them how to make a good story better, or to get an editor to pick up the check for meals, but also to understand the complex and symbiotic relationship between fandom and prodom.

Some of them, like Nick, luck out and find it right away. Some, like Barb, wander into a bunch of Trekkies or Wookies or Beasties who won't read anything except novelizations, who are watchers rather than readers, whose only literary goal is to tell second-hand stories in a third-hand universe, and she wonders what the hell I'm talking about. Then I drag her to a CFG suite or a NESFA party and she meets the fandom *I* know, and suddenly she understands why we keep coming back.

★ ★ ★

So I'm sitting in the airport, waiting to board the plane from Winnipeg to Minnesota. I think there are three mundanes on the flight; everyone else is coming from worldcon. Larry Niven's there, and Connie Willis, and maybe a dozen other pros, and one of the topics of conversation as we await the plane is whose names will make the cover of *Locus* if the plane crashes, and whose names will be in small print on page 37, and how many obituary issues Charlie Brown can get out of it. Then the topic turns to who you would rescue if the plane crashed: Connie and Larry and me, because you wanted more of our stories, or Scott Edelman and me, because you wanted us to be so grateful to you that we'd buy your next twenty stories. (That goes to show you the advantages of being able to do more than one thing well.)

Now, in any other group, that would be a hell of a morbid discussion, but because they were fans, and almost by definition bright and witty, it was the most delightful conversation I'd heard all weekend, and once again I found myself wondering what my life would have been like if Ace had not forwarded that letter to Caz 32 years ago.

And then I thought back to another convention, the 1967 worldcon. I was still very young, and too cynical by half, and when Lester del Rey got up to give his Guest of Honor speech, he looked out at the tables—every worldcon until 1976 presented the GOH speech and the Hugo Awards at a banquet—and said, "Every person in the world that I care for is here tonight."

And I thought: what a feeble thing to say. What a narrow, narrow life this man has lived. What a tiny circle of friends he has.

Well, I've sold 72 books of science fiction—novels, collections, anthologies—and I've won some awards, and I've paid some dues, and I don't think it's totally unrealistic to assume that sometime before I die I will be the Guest of Honor at a worldcon.

I've done a lot with my life (all with Carol's help, to be sure). I've taken several trips to Africa. I've bred 27 champion collies. I've owned and run the second-biggest boarding kennel in the country. I've sired a daughter that any father would be proud to call his own. I've been a lot of places, done a lot of things. I don't think I've led a narrow life at all.

But when I get up to make my Guest of Honor speech, I'll look around the room just the way Lester did, and, because I'm a reasonably honest man, I won't say what he said.

But I *will* say, "With three or four exceptions, every person in the world that I care for is here tonight."

9 781587 150067